They really had only one chance

Bolan crouched and flicked off the massive pistol's safety catch as the helicopter's spotlight blazed into life. Bolan stayed low for the count of three and then rose. His front sight turned black in silhouette against the harsh beam. The helicopter roared in for the kill. The big .50 rolled with recoil in Bolan's hands as he began methodically squeezing the trigger.

Suddenly flame rippled from the chopper's rocket pods. Rockets streaked toward the boat like a swarm of hornets from hell.

Bolan's pistol clacked open on a smoking chamber.

The world ended in orange fire.

MACK BOLAN ®
The Executioner

#243 Assault Reflex
#244 Judas Kill
#245 Virtual Destruction
#246 Blood of the Earth
#247 Black Dawn Rising
#248 Rolling Death
#249 Shadow Target
#250 Warning Shot
#251 Kill Radius
#252 Death Line
#253 Risk Factor
#254 Chill Effect
#255 War Bird
#256 Point of Impact
#257 Precision Play
#258 Target Lock
#259 Nightfire
#260 Dayhunt
#261 Dawnkill
#262 Trigger Point
#263 Skysniper
#264 Iron Fist
#265 Freedom Force
#266 Ultimate Price
#267 Invisible Invader
#268 Shattered Trust
#269 Shifting Shadows
#270 Judgment Day
#271 Cyberhunt
#272 Stealth Striker
#273 UForce
#274 Rogue Target
#275 Crossed Borders
#276 Leviathan
#277 Dirty Mission
#278 Triple Reverse
#279 Fire Wind
#280 Fear Rally

#281 Blood Stone
#282 Jungle Conflict
#283 Ring of Retaliation
#284 Devil's Army
#285 Final Strike
#286 Armageddon Exit
#287 Rogue Warrior
#288 Arctic Blast
#289 Vendetta Force
#290 Pursued
#291 Blood Trade
#292 Savage Game
#293 Death Merchants
#294 Scorpion Rising
#295 Hostile Alliance
#296 Nuclear Game
#297 Deadly Pursuit
#298 Final Play
#299 Dangerous Encounter
#300 Warrior's Requiem
#301 Blast Radius
#302 Shadow Search
#303 Sea of Terror
#304 Soviet Specter
#305 Point Position
#306 Mercy Mission
#307 Hard Pursuit
#308 Into the Fire
#309 Flames of Fury
#310 Killing Heat
#311 Night of the Knives
#312 Death Gamble
#313 Lockdown
#314 Lethal Payload
#315 Agent of Peril
#316 Poison Justice
#317 Hour of Judgment
#318 Code of Resistance

The Executioner
Don Pendleton's®

CODE OF
RESISTANCE

A GOLD EAGLE BOOK FROM
WORLDWIDE®

TORONTO • NEW YORK • LONDON
AMSTERDAM • PARIS • SYDNEY • HAMBURG
STOCKHOLM • ATHENS • TOKYO • MILAN
MADRID • WARSAW • BUDAPEST • AUCKLAND

First edition May 2005
ISBN 0-373-64318-7

Special thanks and acknowledgment to
Chuck Rogers for his contribution to this work.

CODE OF RESISTANCE

Printed in U.S.A.

There is nothing so likely to produce peace as to be
well prepared to meet an enemy.
                    —George Washington 1732–1799

When evil men try to destroy a peaceful society
I will face them head-on. I will raise my own army
to meet their declaration of war.
                                    —Mack Bolan

THE
MACK BOLAN®
LEGEND

Nothing less than a war could have fashioned the destiny of the man called Mack Bolan. Bolan earned the Executioner title in the jungle hell of Vietnam.

But this soldier also wore another name—Sergeant Mercy. He was so tagged because of the compassion he showed to wounded comrades-in-arms and Vietnamese civilians.

Mack Bolan's second tour of duty ended prematurely when he was given emergency leave to return home and bury his family, victims of the Mob. Then he declared a one-man war against the Mafia.

He confronted the Families head-on from coast to coast, and soon a hope of victory began to appear. But Bolan had broken society's every rule. That same society started gunning for this elusive warrior—to no avail.

So Bolan was offered amnesty to work within the system against terrorism. This time, as an employee of Uncle Sam, Bolan became Colonel John Phoenix. With a command center at Stony Man Farm in Virginia, he and his new allies—Able Team and Phoenix Force—waged relentless war on a new adversary: the KGB.

But when his one true love, April Rose, died at the hands of the Soviet terror machine, Bolan severed all ties with Establishment authority.

Now, after a lengthy lone-wolf struggle and much soul-searching, the Executioner has agreed to enter an "arm's-length" alliance with his government once more, reserving the right to pursue personal missions in his Everlasting War.

Washington, D.C.

"Calvin's gone AWOL."

Mack Bolan let the words sink in as he drank coffee and watched the early-morning equestrians riding through the trees along the C & O Canal. His breath steamed the frigid air. He thought about the capital. It balanced some of the worst poverty and racial economic disparity in the U.S. with some of the world's most magnificent monuments, many of which ironically proclaimed, "Equality for All."

All too often the United States had failed to live up to that billing.

The Executioner had fought those failings. Some he had been sent to clean up. Others he had been a part of. But walking through the Beltway with a dusting of snow on the ground and the white spire of the Washington Monument visible above the treetops, one could not help but feel that the intention, however halting and stumbling, was there.

America was about freedom.

Bolan looked at Hal Brognola. "AWOL?" he repeated. "You're saying that he's involved in something and acting without authority?

"Yeah." Brognola shook his head ruefully. Ice skaters were

just starting to make their way down to the frozen canal. "Acting without authority just about covers all the bases."

Bolan shrugged deeper into his pea jacket and sipped his coffee. He owed his life to Calvin James several times over. James had left the Navy a decorated officer with a distinguished record. However, since leaving the Navy, there was very little in the way of authority James answered to other than Stony Man and his own personal code. He was a man whose respect had to be earned.

Bolan considered why Brognola would have asked him for this early-morning meet. Calvin had never been the focal point of a problem before. He was usually the solution. There were certain criminal elements that Calvin James had very little use for. Certain kinds of people he had lost loved ones to. Just like Bolan.

There were certain situations and certain people Bolan would take action against—without hesitation, with or without official sanction—no matter what the consequences. Calvin James was no different. None of the men from Stony Man were.

"You talking within the Lower 48?"

"No." Brognola responded. "Someplace a hell of a lot warmer than here."

Bolan shrugged. "Calvin is a big enough man to choose his battles and pay the consequences." He turned away from the skaters below and locked gazes with Brognola. "But we wouldn't be having this conversation unless there were politics involved."

"There's always politics involved."

"Like I said, Calvin's fought the good fight on every continent on this planet. If he's acting on his own, we both know he has a damn good reason."

"He's your friend, Striker."

"He's your friend, too, Hal." Bolan glanced meaningfully in the direction of the Department of Justice building.

"Yeah. He is." Brognola nodded, looking unhappy. "But rumor has it that our friend is about to get his ass kicked. I'm talking put under the sand without a marker, and on some nameless coconut grove in the South Pacific that no one has ever heard of."

"You want me to go and extract him? Against his will? You've got to be kidding."

Brognola stared at the frozen canal below. The ice was gray in the wan light. "I'd like you…to bring him back before things spiral out of control."

"The South Pacific." Bolan thought about James. "That sounds like some kind of SEAL thing. He owe someone down there?"

"That's the Bear's bet. He did some digging around. He has a full intelligence package waiting for you, if you'll go."

"I can talk to the man. That's all I can promise."

"There's this," Brognola said, pulling an envelope from inside his overcoat.

Bolan took it. "What is it?"

"It's a message. We believe it's from Calvin. It came across a nonsecure radio frequency in Morse code. The signal was broadcast from a Russian military field radio."

Bolan pulled out the paper. The series of numbers at the top were Calvin's current ID code. There was a latitude and longitude, and a very simple message.

I NEED YOU

Below it was Bolan's current Stony Man Farm code. He turned to watch the sunrise. "Any chance of getting the rest of Phoenix to help out?"

"Absolutely under no circumstances. If you accept the mission, you are to go to convince Calvin to extract from the island. No other Stony Man personnel are to be involved. Calvin's status is already questionable. If the whole gang goes down there and gets involved in some kind of Magnificent Seven bullshit, it could risk the future of the entire Farm."

Bolan finished his coffee and wrote a number on the side of the cup.

"I'll go, but if the cause is righteous, I'm more likely to help out than try to hog-tie him and bring him back."

Brognola allowed himself a small smile. He'd read the Bear's intelligence package on what they knew of the situation, and personally, unprofessionally, he'd been hoping Bolan would say that.

Bolan handed the cup to the Man from Justice and walked away.

Brognola read the phone number and recognized it. His smile widened in amused apprehension.

THE SITUATION WAS grim.

Bolan set down the intelligence file and glanced out over the wing at the mist shrouded New Guinea highlands as they began final approach. The battered, ancient and ailing DC10 was barely airworthy, and this was as good as it was going to get.

The minute he stepped off the plane, he would be stepping into a geopolitical shit storm of epic proportions.

He shook his head as he looked down at the file again and began rereading between the lines.

Calvin James could sure as hell pick them.

The Bear had compiled what he could, geographically, anthropologically and politically, and it was sparse.

But it was enough.

The Island of Pa'ahnui was disputed territory, and it was being ripped apart at the seams.

FOR MOST OF ITS HISTORY, Pa'ahnui had been an unspoiled tropical paradise. In 1975 the island came under the loose control of Papua New Guinea, which had become an independent state.

Pa'ahnui was not particularly close to anything on the normal air and sea routes. It was in the classic position of "you can't get there from here."

With tens of thousands of tropical islands throughout the Indonesian Archipelago, fun- and sun-seekers generally stayed on the beaten paths where the beer was cold and the accommodations air-conditioned. In the last half of the twentieth century, only a few hardy sport fisherman and Australian surfers made it to the island, where the outlying coral reefs made for spectacular water sport. They kept their mouths tightly shut about the Garden of Eden they had found.

However, in the late 1990s, an enterprising Australian surveyor on leave had gone rock climbing on some of the inland features, and he had found the traces of the mineral wealth that the island had held secret since its birth. What the surveyor found was something that glittered less than the occasional traces of gold the natives panned for, but it shone with the promise of riches beyond the dreams of avarice.

The tectonic pressures that animated the earth's crust also produced the minerals that had started as a pleasure to man and then became an industrial necessity. The island was made up of five volcanoes. Three were dead, one was dormant and one's semiactive rumblings kept the natives offering flowers and fruit to the idols of their forefathers. Volcanoes were one of the forges of the earth that brought minerals right up to the surface where men could find them literally beneath their feet.

The four river valleys of the island formed a natural dumping ground for the forged minerals of millions of years of volcanic upheaval.

There was trace gold in the creeks. There were diamonds in the deep recesses, but what Pa'ahnui had in staggering abundance was copper, and one had to rip through deliriously vast ribbons of nickel deposits to get to it.

The natives who panned trace gold to make personal adornments were utterly unaware of the untold tons of raw industrial resources beneath their huts.

The serpent had come to Eden.

There were three concentric circles of Pa'ahnui culture. The outer ring was the islanders who lived on the coast and fished. In the interior were four major villages located in the river valleys in the shadow of the volcanoes where the villagers practiced wet rice agriculture. The smallest group was the highlanders, who lived on the fertile, rain-forested sides of the mountains and practiced seminomadic, dry rice agriculture. Quite naturally, the beach dwelling, fishing tribes had received the most exposure to western culture.

And quite naturally, it was they who had sold the island down the river to the Australian Menzies Mining Corporation.

The Menzies Mining Corporation repaved and expanded the abandoned airstrip built during the brief American occupation in WWII and deepened the harbor to allow the docking of freighters. The English mission that had once been the focal point of western civilization on the island now languished in the shadow of the Menzies office building. The natives had no comprehension of the value of what they had, and no idea they had signed away every legal right to their natural resources.

They thought the Australians wished to buy dirt.

Menzies Mining Corporation built a new trading post, and every native who showed up and registered received Menzies

Company scrip worth four thousand Australian dollars, redeemable only at the trading post. The goods available were intriguing: televisions, VCRs, air-conditioning units, stereos, and gasoline-powered generators to make them come to life. The post offered western clothes, cheap jewelry, plasticware and a thousand other things the natives did not need but instantly wanted to have.

They also sold liquor by the case and at enticingly low prices.

When the scrip ran out the Menzies trading post offered credit, which could be paid off in gold dust, or, in manual labor supporting the many building projects that were needed to begin open pit mining on a massive scale. Women whose scrip ran out, or who ran themselves into staggering debt, could embrace the realities of the new economy by working off their spending sprees in other ways in the unofficial company brothel.

The Australian miners began pouring in.

Company housing sprouted up on the beachfronts. In the interior, the natives living on the surveyed sites were told they would have to relocate. More scrip was issued. The leaders of the villages were suitably bribed. Menzies Mining security officers helped deal with any troublemakers. The villages were torn down. The natives were moved to shanties and took menial labor jobs for the miners. The freighters landed, and the earthmoving machines crawled into the interior and began eating the land.

Within three months the first pit was three thousand feet deep and close to three thousand feet wide, and the second was already underway.

The main volcano began rumbling.

As to what happened next, the reports from the Menzies Corporation, the lone police inspector on the island and the locals were contradictory.

What was clear was that a group of miners, on their day off, had gone up into the mountains. They had gone rock climbing. They had gone on a Sunday afternoon diamond-hunting lark. They got good and drunk and, deciding they were tired of the worn out and abused prostitutes in the brothels, had gone to find themselves some fresh highland girls.

Only two of the eight miners made it back down the mountain alive, swearing they had been attacked without provocation by "bloody savages."

Menzies security agents had gone up the mountain to arrest and make an example of the malcontents. Gunfire had been heard, but the agents had never returned.

The police inspector, a sergeant from Brisbane, Australia, had strapped on his .38 service revolver for the second time since his semiretirement to the island. He had mounted his mule and ridden up into the highlands, far beyond his usual jurisdiction, in the general direction the miners claimed to have taken. At the first village he had found the highlanders naked, tending their pigs, smoking hemp and going about their morning routines without a care in the world.

According to his report, the natives had admitted hearing gunfire the previous day but had attributed it to white men hunting wild boar. The inspector had been invited to stay for dinner, being informed by the grinning highlanders that there was leftover pig from the previous night.

The inspector had looked upon the side of meat turning over the spit outside the longhouse and known damn good and well that it was not pig.

He had smoked a bowl of hemp, taken a coconut shell of what the highlanders passed for tea, thanked them for their cooperation and hospitality, mounted his mule and got off the mountain.

A few days later a group of four surveyors working the interior were found dead in their tents.

It was war.

The Papua New Guinean government was more than willing to let Pa'ahnui be scraped flat. They wanted the potential billions in hard currency the mining would bring. They had declared to the outside world that there were Communist insurgents on the island. A group of natives declared the Island of Pa'ahnui an independent democratic republic. A very small subcommittee of the United Nations debated what was to be done. Meanwhile dynamite was stolen from the mining camps and trucks, and bridges and other Menzies Corporation assets began exploding. The insurrection spread like wildfire. Menzies security agents leaving the safety of the coast were overwhelmed and slaughtered.

In the past year the Menzies Mining Corporation had thrown up its hands at any chance of a profitable resolution and sold their share of the mining rights to the multinational Craig Consortium. At Craig's suggestion the government of Papua New Guinea had instigated a naval blockade, and all news and information coming out of the island had ceased.

This brought Bolan back to the Calvin James situation.

The Phoenix Force commando was a former Navy SEAL, and Aaron Kurtzman "The Bear" had delved deep into his service records. When James had been in the SEALs he had participated in a goodwill, cross-training liaison with the Australian SAS. Australia had administered Papua New Guinea at one time. To this day there continued to be small ugly incidents along the border between New Guinea and Indonesia, which was swiftly becoming a vastly overpopulated archipelago. Indonesia gazed hungrily on the vast, sparsely inhabited New Guinea interior and the rumors of her rich and unexploited mineral wealth. The Indonesians fostered revolutionary movements in New Guinea, and her Special Forces regularly made incursions across the border. Elements of the

Australian SAS lurked on that border, training the natives to defend themselves and intercept Indonesian infiltrators.

The Australian government vigorously denied that the SAS, assisted by local elements, frequently crossed the border engaging in aggressive counterinterdiction missions.

The U.S. Navy had "vacationed" Calvin James in Papua New Guinea. His mission, with a few other selected SEALs, had been to help the Australian SAS train Papua New Guinea soldiers in underwater infiltration and demolition techniques.

One of the men he had trained had been from the outer islands.

Hose Sh'sho had returned to his island after his service as a native auxiliary attached to the Australian SAS. James had once gone to the island on leave before the trouble had begun.

The best that Kurtzman could figure was that Sh'sho had put out a call for help out about a month ago. Calvin James had received it and disappeared.

Forty-eight hours ago, in a three second radio broadcast, James had called out to Bolan for help.

The Triple Witch

Stephen Craig was a sociopath.

He knew it.

He embraced it.

Craig turned his head.

The four, jet-black Neapolitan mastiffs lying near his desk snapped to attention. The huge animals had learned very early in their lives to observe and obey their master's slightest movement. The chrome spikes on their leather collars gleamed, as did their disturbingly blue eyes. Their vocal cords had been so modified they could not bark. It was not part of their job description. They were not guard dogs.

They were weapons.

Craig nodded once at his animals. "Good dogs."

The four mastiffs shuddered with equal measures of pleasure and relief and settled back down with their heads on their paws.

Craig glanced out the panoramic window of his office suite. Wind and rain lashed the windows and the sea outside was a heavy chop. The twin hulls of the gigantic, catamaran slid through the waves like a pair of knives. The motor yacht was fully 250 long. It had been built to Craig's personal specifications and had been described in the media as an "ocean-going monstrosity."

The Triple Witch had a number of unique design features that the media had never dreamed of.

The door to Craig's office slid open. A woman entered with catlike silence to her steps. Her eyes were brown with golden motes deep within. This matched her golden brown deepwater tan and the highlights in her brown hair. The woman seemed to have been poured from molten bronze.

Sculptured sinew fought with feminine curves across her flesh in a glorious war in which both sides had claimed victory. Jaguars in the jungles of South America would have envied the way the woman could ripple across a room. She wore only biking shorts and a sports bra. Her golden brown skin gleamed with a light sheen of sweat.

A deeper light glowed in her eyes.

Her hands were taped and bloodied.

The Triple Witch had a fully equipped gymnasium, but on long ocean voyages the woman's favorite form of physical exercise was fighting with Craig's bodyguards in a round-robin orgy of just-less-than-crippling, hand-to-hand violence.

On the Craig Consortium payroll, her job description was personal assistant.

But she was Craig's chief bodyguard.

She was also his chauffeur, private pilot, personal trainer, arms instructor, tactical adviser and concubine. Craig came as close to trusting her as he was capable of trusting another human being.

The woman was well aware of the fact that Craig was a sociopath and had no problem with it.

She examined a bloody fist and smiled. "I hear things are heating up on the island."

Craig smiled. She loved to oversimplify. "Yes, apparently Shootie's been eliminated."

"So that leaves Ilya." The woman smirked derisively. "In command."

Craig nodded. "That is the current situation."

The woman pulled off her bra and tossed it unceremoniously onto the head of Caesar, the second mastiff from the left. The massive dog let out small sigh, but his head lay unmoving beneath the undergarment.

Stephen Craig was a billionaire. He could buy any pleasure he wanted, no matter how heinous or illegal, on any corner of the earth and get away with it. Still, the woman before him continued to teach him things about himself.

"You know Ilya doesn't obey orders worth shit. He's going to mess things up worse than they already are." She was getting angry.

Craig nodded. "He just doesn't know me well enough to know any better."

"And the natives, they've been getting help from somebody recently," the woman said. "A professional."

"I've an idea about that," Craig replied.

The woman stripped off her clinging Lycra shorts. She stood naked and gleaming before him. She left the bloody tape in place on her hands. Her smile turned feral. "This should be good," she murmured.

Craig was not entirely sure which of three imminent activities she was referring to. "We're about forty-eight hours out from Suriname. I have business there," he said. "Tomorrow, when we're in range off the coast, I want you to take the helicopter. There is something I want you to do."

Falamae, Solomon Islands

"CAN'T GET THERE from here."

Truman Hitihiti was five feet eleven inches and 350

pounds of muscle in a XXXL Oakland Raider tank top and a
sarong. Traditional Polynesian warriors' tattoos covered his
arms like sleeves and his exposed knees and calves like socks.
His skull-clinging Afro was dyed an implausible platinum
blond, as were his short Vandyke and eyebrows. He shrugged
shoulder muscles the size of cantaloupes in dismissal of the
subject and lit himself a blunt.

Bolan had gotten the dossier on the man from Kurtzman
and the lowdown from his local contact. Hitihiti had been
born on Tonga, but his parents had moved to Hawaii when he
was a young man. As a teenager he had gotten into trouble
with the local youth gangs in Honolulu. But the services of
Truman "The Human Wall" Hitihiti had been proved so valu-
able in the noseguard position for the high school football
team that his extracurricular activities and low grade point average had been largely ignored. They did, however, get in the
way of his getting into college. A judge had given Hitihiti a
choice of the United States Army or jail. He had traded on
his local football heroics to get recruited straight into the
Military Police. Within two years he was facing multiple
charges of conspiracy, trafficking in contraband and racket-
eering. Little could be proved, but marijuana had been found
in his possession and he had been dishonorably discharged.

In the meantime, his connections had been made.

Hawaii was too hot for him, but he was already involved in
smuggling in the Philippines. In off-seasons, he had wrestled
professionally in Japan and was rumored to have done some
gunrunning with the Yakuza through the Okinawan Islands.
Truman Hitihiti became very adept at smuggling and set himself up in business. He specialized in trafficking among the
Polynesian Islands, but he would take anything, anywhere, for
the right price. Sometime, during one of his weapons runs in

Okinawa, he had come into Trevor Burdick's orbit of operations.

Hitihiti currently kept his business south of the equator. As smugglers went, he was fairly reliable.

"Oh c'mon." Bolan smiled at the smuggler. "It's only three hundred kilometers to Pa'ahnui. It's a piece of cake."

"Cake? Pa'ahnui's under blockade." Truman shook his head decisively. "No one goes there."

"Lot's of people go there," Bolan said. "Besides, their patrol boats are thirty years old, and they only have two of them."

"You know something? You got that positive, can-do, white-man attitude. That shit conquered the world. I admire that a lot." The smell of marijuana and tobacco filled the little shack on the pier as Hitihiti waved his hand for emphasis at his docked boat. "But they got 40 mm cannons, man. Blow my shit right out of the water. Sink me to the bottom. Davey Jones's locker, all that bad shit."

A bass voice rumbled low and threatening behind the smuggler. "Truman, you are so goddamn fat no one's sinking your ass anyplace."

Truman Hitihiti's huge frame nearly levitated off his bar stool. He clasped his chest as if he might have a heart attack. He clearly had mixed feelings about the man suddenly casting his shadow over him. "Big Red!"

Trevor Burdick loomed over the smuggler like a tree. Hitihiti had about forty-five pounds on the redheaded ex-Marine, but Burdick had a good six inches in height. He leaned down nearly nose to nose with the Tongan. "Your ass floats, Truman. You know what I'm saying to you? You're a floater. I'm saying leave the poi alone. You've had enough."

"Aw, shit, man..." Hitihiti seemed to shrivel unhappily in his seat.

Burdick plucked the blunt from Hitihiti's fingers. "Thanks, Truman. Don't mind if I do."

"Jesus." The smuggler sagged back against the bar and rolled his eyes unhappily at Bolan. "You with him? Big Red?" He shook his head ruefully. "Bad medicine."

"A left-handed Gemini with a bad moon rising," agreed Burdick. He handed back the blunt. "Don't ever forget that, Truman."

Hitihiti took a long, huge hit to calm his nerves.

"So, Truman." Bolan looked directly at him. "Can you get us to Pa'ahnui?"

"You know somethin', man? I knew you was no American ex-patriot, moment I saw you. Ex-pat's go ugly real fast in the Solomons. You're all crisp and clean, you a nasty smooth bastard." He pointed an accusing finger. "And you ain't no reporter if you're with Big Red." The Tongan's eyes shot back and forth between the two very dangerous-looking white men with grave suspicion. "What you want to go to Pa'ahnui for, anyway? That island's all fucked up. Fighting like savages. What you gonna do there? The Russians got all the guns they need. The natives got nothing but coconuts. They ain't buying nothin'. No profit to be made there, brah. No one doin' nothin' on Pa'ahnui but dying."

"I have a friend there," Bolan said.

"You have a friend there?" Truman scowled. "And how much cargo we talking about your friend wanting?"

Bolan turned to Burdick. "You get what I asked for?"

Burdick shook his head. He had once been a minor but significant figure on the Asian black market weapons scene. That was until he had run afoul of Mack Bolan in Korea. Bolan had slapped Burdick onto the right side of the line. Since that time, Bolan had called upon the ex-Force Recon Marine to serve his country on several occasions. Particularly when he had needed a deniable one-man goon squad with an idiot savant's grasp of languages.

"It's been awhile since I've been in the game. You know that." Burdick looked at Bolan with vague accusation. "Most of my old contacts are dead, retired or in jail. You asked for AKs." The big man shrugged. "This is what I could get on short notice from an old English ex-pat buddy from back in the day."

Burdick opened a battered canvas duffel bag at his feet and pulled out a wad of phosphate finished sheet steel. He yanked out a telescoping wire stock and clicked the foregrip into place. The mess of metal stampings suddenly appeared to be a submachine gun.

Hitihiti pointed a thick finger. "French MAT-49."

"No, Vietnamese," corrected Burdick. "But close, Truman, real close. When the French folded in Indochina, they left thousands of these rods behind. The Vietnamese took them and converted them to the Tokarev pistol round. Just as sturdy, just as reliable, higher velocity. I have a hundred of them on the airstrip, each with six spare magazines, web gear and ten thousand rounds of ammo. It's not an AK, but if you're arming illiterate savages who've never fired a shot in anger, this'll be as good a place to start as any."

"Not bad," Bolan admitted. "What about that light support I asked for?"

Burdick folded up the submachine gun and slid it back into his bag. "I got two 90 mm recoilless rifles left over from when Uncle Sam failed to cowboy up over there, and two Chinese Type 63-1 60 mm pack mortars, ammo for both, and ten RPG-7s. I'm telling you, the Vietnamese are selling all their old stuff at bargain prices. They are genuinely joining the goddamn free world economy."

"You white boys are starting a revolution!" Hitihiti said.

"The revolution on Pa'ahnui has already started," Bolan replied. "I'm just going there to pick up a friend. But if that fails, Plan B is to win the revolution."

The Tongan folded arms as thick as hams across his chest defiantly. "Okay, so, tell me, brah. I want to do this for you because?"

The question hung in the air between them in the haze of smoke.

"Well. I got this." Bolan reached into the breast pocket of his shirt and pulled out a thick roll of U.S. hundred-dollar bills. "And I got this…" He reached into another pocket and pulled out a money clip loaded with Australian notes. "And…hmm." Bolan dug deep into his khaki shorts. "This." A two-inch-thick sheaf of Papuan Kina notes flapped onto the bar. "Oh, and this." Bolan rolled a crumpled, fist-sized wad of Indonesian rupiahs held together by a rubberband onto the bar.

"That's what I got."

Truman Hitihiti's eyes were red-veined from the marijuana, but they focused with cold precision on the piles of colorful currency on top of the bar and noted their relative thickness as he did the math. He pointed at the U.S. dollars. "I like those. Green is so soothing, man. Cures your ills. Calms everyone's shit."

Bolan pushed the roll of hundreds over to the Tongan. "Me, Red and our cargo. On the beach. Pa'ahnui. Seventy-two hours." Bolan took the remaining mass of money and shoved it back into his pockets. "The rest as a bonus, once I have my toes in the sand."

Burdick leaned over the bar again. "What do ya say, Truman?"

Truman Hitihiti made the C-notes disappear into his sarong. He stared woefully across the waters. "I shoulda never have left Tonga."

"YOU WERE RIGHT."

The woman on the beach examined the faces of the men at the bar of the little pier-side shack through binoculars as she spoke into her cell phone. "Money is changing hands."

The South Pacific was vast, with tens of thousands of tiny islands, but many were separated by vast amounts of ocean. The majority did not have airstrips. Few had decent harbors. The farther a person got from the huge archipelagos, the fewer ways there were to get anywhere from anywhere.

It had been a very good bet that operators assisting the natives on Pa'ahnui would try to insert from the Solomon Islands. The Solomons had six major islands and hundreds of inhabited smaller ones. Sixteen airfields serviced the entire nation. It was not hard to arrange a lookout at each one and find out when a private cargo plane had landed. It had taken only a few beers and a few hundred-dollar bills in the right places to find out who ran the thin and incompetent gauntlet of the Papuan blockade.

"How many?" Craig asked.

"Three, one is the Hitihiti guy the locals talked about. He's a Polynesian, a smuggler. He's worked throughout the South Pacific, but he specializes in the Indonesian and Polynesian archipelagos. The other two are Caucasians. Big. The redhead came in on a cargo plane from Australia, talks like an American and he's got cargo, a lot of it. The crates are the right size and quantity to be weapons and ammunition. He bribed his way past the customs inspector. The third one…" She frowned as she observed the dark haired man with the startling blue eyes. "He appeared out of nowhere."

"Impressions?"

"Hitihiti looks like his reputation. He's a scumbag, but probably as tough as they say. The redhead is even bigger, and looks U.S. military. Probably a Marine by the way he swaggers. The third one…" The woman's eyes narrowed apprecia-tively. "That one is an operator. You can tell by the way he moves."

"Just the two?"

"That is all our informants have detected."

Craig calculated. "If it's an arms shipment, they could be advisers and instructors."

"That would be my guess," the woman concurred. "You want me to sic customs on them?"

"No, let them set sail. Let them get within sight of their objective."

The woman had a lovely smile, but a man with any sense of self-preservation would have cringed if he had seen the look in her eyes. "Then we drop the hammer," she said.

"Exactly," Craig agreed. "Any mistakes, you know Plan B."

"Mm." The woman lay back in the sand as the sun ham-mered her golden body with equatorial rays. "I know Plan B."

3

Suriname

Rutger Eugenius Rutgers poured himself two fingers of ten-year-old single malt whisky. The rain lashed the beach outside, and the wind moaned and rattled the windowpanes of his nineteenth-century Dutch farmhouse. A fire crackled in the fireplace of his study. Rutgers stared out into the middle distance. He had done well for himself.

Most mercenaries didn't.

The fact was a lot of mercs died in unnamable shit holes. More retired to geographically different but socially identical shit holes whose only saving grace was that no one there specifically wanted to kill them.

Rutgers had done all right.

He was one of three CEOs in a company of his own founding. He took pride in the fact that in a small but significant way his company influenced the outcome of world events. Rutgers lived on beachfront property in a tropical South American paradise. A paradise far and away from the frozen, flooded Frisian Islands of his birth. He was married to a beautiful woman and had three even more beautiful mistresses in Paramaribo, Amsterdam and Paris. He had gotten out of the lead-swapping end of merc work relatively unscathed. He felt the ache of major wounds only on his occasional visits to Paris in winter.

He was a multimillionaire.

Rutgers sipped his whisky, looked at the lightning-lashed ocean and became intimately aware that someone had gotten past his dogs, his servants, his bodyguards and his security suite and was now in the study with him.

Rutgers casually swirled the ice in his glass, and without looking away from the storm outside his window considered the distance between himself and the freshly cleaned, oiled, loaded and locked Browning Hi-Power pistol inches from his left hand on the desk. A voice spoke from his favorite leather chair directly behind him.

"Don't even think about it."

Rutgers took another sip of his whisky and rolled it around on his tongue. It was quite likely the last drink he would ever enjoy. He took a moment to savor the taste before he replied. "I already told you I wasn't interested. Which part of that did you not understand?"

Rutgers turned slowly, prepared to throw the heavy, cut crystal glass and dive across the desk, scooping up his pistol as he lunged.

But those thoughts left his mind as he faced his opponent.

Stephen Craig sat comfortably in his chair.

The billionaire reached into his coat to produce a Cuban cigar and a lighter. He bit the tip from the cigar and spit it on Rutgers's Persian rug. The lighter flamed, and Craig took several long draws. He blew three smoke rings and speared a thin stream of smoke through all three.

Rutgers was impressed, but he kept most of his attention on the dogs.

There were four of them. Their coats were black, but in the firelight he could see the wet, dark-stained matting of blood on their muzzles. Craig's dogs had killed his. Rutgers did not wish to speculate on the condition of his guards. Eight blue eyes glowed at him unblinkingly in the orange light of the fireplace. Their attention never wavered. The immense animals vibrated with intensity as their eyes followed the whisky glass to lips and then back down again.

Rutgers had faced death more times than he cared to count. This time, it had caught him unprepared.

"I found your answer unacceptable," Craig said.

Rutgers stared into the eyes of a maniac and prepared himself for death. "I don't care," he stated.

Craig poured himself a finger of Rutgers's whisky with water and no ice. "Why not?"

Rutgers flared. "Because you have—"

The Dutchman very slowly lowered his finger. At his tone of voice the four mastiffs had come to their feet.

"Because you have a goddamn revolution on your hands." Rutgers shook his head. "It will end in tears, man. You should pull out while you can." Rutgers had seen these no win situations before. It wasn't worth the effort.

"But I've invested too much time and money into the project to pull out," Craig replied. "I do not wish to pull out."

"So you've come back to me, again. Why?"

"Well, I went with a man you know, Kliivland. He asked me to ask you again."

"Schutte?" Rutgers grunted noncommittally. "I gather he is having a rough time of it, then."

"Schutte's dead."

"Ah." Rutgers polished off his whisky but retained the glass in his hand. "And who is in command now?"

"Ilya."

"Ilya? Ilya Gaz?" Rutgers stared in disbelief. "Why didn't you just send Attila the Hun, then, and be done with it!"

"Attila wasn't available. Ilya was." Craig shrugged. "And you said no."

"You're goddamned right I said no!" Rutgers prepared himself for the worst. His fingers tightened around the glass. He considered the pistol on the desk again, as well as the Napoleanic cavalry saber mounted on the wall. "And I still do."

"Mm." Craig nodded. "Well, perhaps we should call a shareholders meeting."

"A what...shareholders?" Rutgers had founded Executive Options. There were only three shareholders, all equal partners. Himself, an Englishman and a South African. He had fought alongside the other two men in Angola more years ago than he cared to remember. "Nigel is in London, and last I heard Artemus is touring—"

"India with his wife," Craig said, finishing the sentence. Craig. "They aren't shareholders anymore. I bought them out."

Rutgers's knuckles went white around his glass. "Are they still breathing?"

"Oh, yes. I simply made your partners offers they couldn't refuse." Craig took a long pull on his cigar. "Financial and otherwise."

The Dutchman's cheeks flexed in barely restrained rage. "They told me nothing of this."

"Well, it was quite sudden, and keeping the information privileged added another zero to their checks."

Rutgers's shoulders sank. "My friends."

"You friends are mercenaries. They don't work for love. They work for money." Craig leaned back in the chair and put his feet up on Rutgers's desk. "Now you work for me."

Pa'ahnui

INSPECTOR FILMOORE OILED his submachine gun.

Most of its green paint was missing. To the untrained eye, it looked more like a piece of junk than a firearm. The weapon had been manufactured in 1945, the same year the inspector had been born.

He had carried a weapon exactly like it during the war in Vietnam.

The inspector glanced up at the sound of another burst of automatic rifle fire that was followed by a woman's screams. He had not particularly liked Shutte Kliivland, but at least the South African had kept a rein on the Menzies security agents and the Russian thugs that had mostly replaced them. The South African commander had kept the violence mostly between his men and the rebels, though the interior was rife with stories of atrocities against the inland villages. He had made a polite pretense of respecting the inspector's position on the island.

Two nights ago, the South African had been found outside his command shack with his head blown from his shoulders, and Ilya had assumed command.

The Russian savage was staging a bloody pogrom against the natives.

Filmoore loved Pa'ahnui. He had escaped life on his father's sheep station by joining the army as soon as they would take him. As a young man, he had managed to escape from the Australian participation in the Vietnam conflict relatively unscathed. He and some mates he'd made during the war had subsequently set out on a sailboat and traveled in the South Pacific for a few years. They had come upon Pa'ahnui, and Filmoore had fallen in love with the volcanic isle. The fishing had been spectacular. So had the surfing. After an initial period of aloofness, the soft-spoken natives became friendly.

Filmoore had returned to Australia and become a policeman. Each year on his leaves, he had returned to the unspoiled island of his dreams. The years had passed. He'd been married and widowed. Filmoore considered the prospect of growing old, alone, in Brisbane, and found it untenable. He'd made friends in Pa'ahnui. He knew the English missionaries well. The missionaries had written a letter, as had some of the local big men. They wanted a police inspector on the island.

They wanted Patrick Filmoore.

His mates on the Brisbane force had proclaimed him the luckiest man alive. Filmoore had been issued a .38 revolver, a field radio, a pair of binoculars, and surprisingly, as the sole face of Australian sovereignty on the island, an Owen submachine gun.

When Pa'ahnui had switched over to Papuan rule, no one had seen any reason to replace Filmoore.

He had drawn his revolver only once in his years of duty, and that had been on a nonnative. Except for one magazine fired into the air on the queen's birthday each year, the Owen never left its crate.

The inspector was well liked on Pa'ahnui. He had learned the local language, he was a decent fisherman, he gave good gifts. He had demonstrated the good sense to marry a local girl, and he did not get involved in local feuds or altercations unless he had been specifically asked to. His arbitration was regarded as generally fair and impartial.

Coastal fishing clans, inland tribesman and even the highlanders all agreed. Inspector Filmoore was smarter than the average white man.

Then Menzies Mining had come. Their liquor and company scrip had come. The earthmovers had come, followed by the security agents, the Papuan naval blockade and finally the Russian scourge. The people he was sworn to protect had begged Filmoore to take action.

He had contacted the capitol. He had written the Australian consulate. The violence had escalated, and nothing had been done. The government in Port Moresby was not concerned about what happened on Pa'ahnui, as long the flow of ore continued without disruption.

The only thing Filmoore had managed to do was to send his wife off to the mainland before the blockading ships had arrived.

The inspector was alone.

He knew he could not stand up to the Russians in a gunfight. Time had been kind to him, but he was an old man. The Russians had heavy weapons, numerical superiority, and they would cut him down in the street in seconds. Yet, long ago, thousands of miles away, in a place called Phuoc Toy, Inspector Filmoore had been Corporal Filmoore, Forward Scout for the Royal Australian Artillery. In that place, he had become intimately familiar with a weapon exactly like the one he held now. In that same place, he had also become intimately familiar with the act of lurking in the jungle.

The Owen gun was out of its crate.

Inspector Filmoore checked the loads in his .38 Webley service revolver and strapped on his Sam Browne belt. He had spent the past hour sawing the barrels of his shotgun down to the fore end. The previous day he had buried the ammunition he could not carry on his person a thousand meters outside the village. He packed a collapsible fishing rod, a spare set of clothes, his Sykes-Fairbairn commando dagger, six loaded magazines for the Owen, a net hammock and a few tins of meat into a knapsack and figured he was as ready as he was ever going to be.

The inspector put on his battered old digger hat and slipped out the back door of his house.

Gunfire echoed in the near distance. Flames glowed orange through the trees, and thick plumes of smoke obscured the stars. The Russians were driving from village to village in heavily armed jeeps looting and pillaging like invading Mongols. The inspector's jaw tightened.

American law enforcement had a motto he'd always admired.

To protect and serve.

Inspector Patrick Filmoore shouldered his Owen gun and nodded at the kelpie curled up at the foot of the bed. Blue stared back up at him and wrinkled his brows.

"Come."

Blue rose, stretched and followed his master as Filmoore went out the back door of his house and faded into the trees.

4

The raindrops fell like warm fists onto the *Bread and Butter*. Truman Hitihiti's boat looked like a dilapidated extra from a low budget pirate movie, but he had dropped his sails when the squall had set in and the twin diesels beneath the water-line hammered the ancient shrimper through the waves with surprising efficiency.

Truman knew something about getting from point A to point B in the South Pacific.

Hitihiti's first mate was a perennially drunken Solomon Islander of indeterminate late middle age named Beaver. But Beaver, to his credit, was a whiz with a wok over a ten-brick barbecue pit. Breakfast and lunch were sashimi and sliced toasted breadfruit. Dinner was catch of the moment stir-fried with rice, coconut milk, curry and peppers.

Thunder rolled, and lightning crashed in the distance as the summer squall gained momentum.

It appeared that Beaver was an able seaman and had spent most of his life on the ocean. He was the first to sit up from their meal beneath a shelter half on the foredeck, and cock his head, judging the thunder.

"That no thunder, Cap'n."

Hitihiti glanced up from under the tarp, squinting into the warm South Pacific summer rain. The sun was setting behind the blackened and bruised clouds. "What do you hear?" he asked.

Bolan set down his chopsticks. "Helicopters."

Burdick shoved his supper away and shrugged a 90 mm recoilless rifle onto his shoulder. He peered into the gloom as he flicked the lens caps from the optical sight. "Truman, does the Papuan navy have choppers?"

"Some tired old Hueys, maybe." Hitihiti reached under his bench and pulled out a brutally shortened FN assault rifle. "But nothing they could land on one of their patrol boats."

"They're coming up behind us, from the east." Bolan raised his laser range-finding binoculars. "And it isn't a Huey."

The Aérospatiale Dauphin was a beautiful helicopter. It had a very clean airframe and agile flight characteristics. For a nonmilitary helicopter, it was capable of sustained high speed and had good range.

Bolan grimly noted the rocket pods beneath the two lateral armament pylons.

Red squinted into his optical sight. "Range me."

Bolan pressed a button on his binoculars. "He's holding at 650 meters. What's your range with that?"

"Effective? Four hundred meters. Practical..." Red braced himself on the rolling deck of the boat. Rain ran down his face. "Two thousand from a stable platform on a nonmoving target."

Hitihiti rammed his throttles forward.

"Uh...stable platform?" Red shouted.

The helicopter's nose dipped as it began to follow them.

"Nonmoving target..." Red shook his head. "Well, just...shit! Fire in the hole!" The 90 mm recoilless rifle belched fire from both ends. The helicopter swerved, and the high-explosive armor-piercing shell streaked into the night. Red unlocked his smoking breech and reached for another shell. "This ain't gonna work!"

Bolan agreed, but raised his M-4 carbine and began firing short bursts.

The helicopter was staying out of range.

Red raised the 90 mm rifle again. "Try this!"

The antitank weapon boomed again but at a higher pitch. In the distance, the helicopter lit up with hundreds of yellow spark flashes. The Dauphin banked abruptly and swung out into the gathering darkness.

"Yeah." Red lowered the smoking tube from his shoulder and glowered after the retreating aircraft. "Come back anytime."

Bolan smiled. "Beehive?"

"Yeah, I gave him about a thousand .17-caliber antipersonnel fléchettes. At that range, if I was even close, I figured he'd have to take some of the pattern. Problem is, at that range, I doubt if even one of those darts pierced his fuselage. With luck, we've scared the shit out of him. If he's one of those bound and determined kind of assholes, he'll be back and he'll be pissed."

"Beaver! Take the helm!" Hitihiti stomped across the deck cradling an M-60 general-purpose machine gun. He mounted the weapon on a metal post sticking up from the stern deck and racked the action. He unslung his rifle and handed it to Bolan. "Here, brah, more range."

Bolan took the rifle and scanned the gloom as the wind and rain whipped the waves. The sun had dipped below the horizon and the black clouds left the Solomon Sea in a rain-drenched darkness "He's watching us."

"Son of a bitch." Red plucked open his red-hot breech and sucked his singed fingers. Raindrops sizzled on the tube. He slid in a fresh shell, slammed the action shut and locked it. "He's watching us? Let's get a good look at him."

Red tilted his weapon skyward. "Show time!"

Orange fire bloomed fore and aft of the weapon. Bolan and Hitihiti waited with their weapons ready. A moment later the stormy night lit up as Red's illumination round detonated.

In the burning magnesium glare, the helicopter appeared six hundred yards aft.

Hitihiti began hammering on full-auto, red tracers streaking out, clawing for the helicopter. Bolan took an extra second to adjust for the wind and the rolling deck and squeezed the trigger. The rifle bucked and the fuselage of the distant helicopter sparked. Bolan kept his front sight steady and began rapidly squeezing the trigger.

The helicopter stayed on station and took the hits.

Fire rippled beneath the Dauphin's weapons pylons.

"Beaver!" Hitihiti roared over the sound of the storm and his own weapon. "Hard to starboard!"

The *Bread and Butter* surged with surprising nimbleness, turning as the 12-round salvo of 68 mm rockets hammered the surf. Spumes of ocean erupted skyward as they detonated in the vessel's wake. The helicopter swung off, nose down, burning to put distance between itself and the boat. Even with Red's illumination round burning in the sky like a small angry sun, the chopper swiftly disappeared into the night.

Bolan stared into the storm. The pilot was good, but it was quite clear he was not a trained gunship pilot. If he had known what he was doing, he would have gone to high altitude and destroyed them with a single diving attack. It appeared he did not know how to shoot and scoot at the same time.

"Truman, how far are we from Pa'ahnui?"

"Not far, brah!" The Tongan kept hunkered behind his machine gun scanning the skies. The illumination round was swiftly descending from the sky. It hit the waves a hundred yards aft, sizzling and hissing as it began to descend below the waves.

Blackness fell across them like a blanket.

Bolan slipped a fresh magazine into his rifle. "You got any more illumination rounds, Red?"

"Down in the hold, crated away, somewhere."

"I suggest you go find one, and fast."

Red squeezed his bulk down the steps and disappeared into the hold.

Hitihiti's voice growled reprovingly. "You got me in some real shit, ."

"Yeah." Bolan peered into the night. He counted the seconds between lightning flashes and thunderclaps and strained to pick up the sound of rotors.

Bolan raised his ear to the rain, listening. "Here he comes."

Rotors hammered in the blackness.

"From where?" Hitihiti swung his weapon, searching for a target.

"Red." Bolan flicked his selector to full-auto. "I need you."

The sound of the rotors overpowered the sound of thunder. The chopper was closing fast.

"Red!"

"I'm coming!" The big man's shoes slapped the rickety steps as he pounded up out of the hold. "I'm—"

The illumination round was unnecessary. The chopper's spotlight suddenly lit up the *Bread and Butter* like the sun. The chopper was two hundred yards out, just above the waves and throwing rooster tails of ocean in its rotor wake. Bolan leaned out over the rail and began shooting.

The helicopter was closing straight at the *Bread and Butter*'s prow.

"Beaver!" The bridge was directly between the chopper and Truman's weapon. "Beaver! Hard to—"

Beaver and the bridge of the *Bread and Butter* detonated

in orange flame. The ship shuddered, and the searing blast threw Bolan over the rail. A black wave slapped him beneath the surface and his rifle slipped from his hands. Bolan descended a few feet and held position as the surface above continued to light up in orange flashes. He kicked to the surface as the chopper roared past, its rocket run finished.

The *Bread and Butter* was burning. Bolan grabbed the rail and pulled himself aboard. The blast had knocked Hitihiti to the stern rail where he sat stunned with his scalp split open.

"Red!"

Burdick's head popped up from the hold somewhat blackened and singed. "Fuck this!" he shouted.

Red was all right.

"Where's the 90?" Bolan asked.

Red looked around himself. "I—shit!"

"Truman!" Bolan went to the M-60. "Get up!"

Hitihiti heaved himself to his feet. His eyes rolled back in his head, and he promptly sat down again. Bolan spun the gun on its mount and found it hopelessly jammed.

The helicopter was banking hard, preparing to make its second rocket run.

"Red! Get Truman out of here! Abandon ship!" Bolan drew his Desert Eagle.

Red ripped some ancient looking orange life vests from a deck locker and picked up the massive Tongan with a groan. He stared at Bolan and his pistol, then tossed a vest at his feet. "Jesus Christ, c'mon! There's nothing more you can—"

"Move!" Bolan roared.

Burdick and Hitihiti went over the side.

Bolan took his pistol in a two-handed grip and fixed his gaze on the glowing tritium spot of his front sight.

There was one last thing he had to do. They had to abandon ship. Only dumb luck had kept the high-explosive mortar and cannon munitions belowdecks from detonating on the first run. The next run would burn the *Bread and Butter* to her waterline if it didn't blow her to bits. But once they abandoned ship, the helicopter could circle at its leisure. The pilot would strafe them until all three of them were greasy red stains dispersing in the storm.

They had only one chance.

Bolan crouched and flicked off the massive pistol's safety catch.

The helicopter's spotlight blazed into life. Bolan stayed low for the count of three, then rose. His front sight turned black in silhouette against the harsh beam. The helicopter roared in for the kill. The big .50-caliber pistol rolled with recoil in Bolan's hands as he methodically began squeezing the trigger.

With his fifth shot, the spotlight suddenly winked out.

Flame rippled from the rocket pods, and rockets streaked toward the *Bread and Butter* like a swarm of hornets from hell, borne on wings of smoke and fire.

Bolan's pistol clacked open on a smoking empty chamber. The world ended in orange fire.

THE WRECKAGE WAS swiftly burning out. The woman scanned the choppy surface for signs of life, but concentrated her attention outside the flickering glow of the fading flames. The surface was a roiling black caldron. The helicopter shuddered as the storm worsened. The engine was making a whining noise it was not supposed to. The wind whistled through bullet holes in the windscreen. The copilot was staring hard at a number of red lights blinking on his controls and kept shooting meaningful looks at the woman in the left seat.

Craig's voice spoke over the radio. "Did you get him?"

"The boat is destroyed," the woman confirmed.

"Survivors?"

"Can't tell." She continued to search the waves with her binoculars, but the situation was problematic at best. "The asshole shot out my spotlight."

"You should have gotten night-vision equipment."

"There was no time. We barely got the helicopter to the Solomons and unloaded in time to catch up with them. We'll proceed to the island and sweep again tomorrow."

"Belay that. Do you have any rockets left?"

The woman checked her weapons suite display. "Yes, thirty-six."

"Expend your rockets in a pattern around the wreckage."

The woman smiled. She enjoyed firing the rockets.

She could tell that Craig was smiling as he spoke on the other side of the line. "Then proceed to the island and begin the next phase."

5

Big Red was right.

Truman Hitihiti was a floater. The huge man was positively buoyant. Once freed from the embrace of the surf, however, the titanic Tongan turned into 350 pounds of poi and was just as cumbersome. The Executioner groaned with effort as he wrestled Hitihiti's inert form onto the sand like a beached whale.

Bolan collapsed from fatigue. He sat in the surf and leaned against Hitihiti's mass, simply letting the waves wash over his feet as he concentrated on the normally automatic process of breathing. He had come upon the Tongan quite by accident in the pearly light of the predawn. The Tongan had been bobbing gently in the waves, an unconscious life buoy.

Red was nowhere to be seen.

Bolan finally summoned the strength to throw an elbow into the Tongan's ribs to see if he could rouse him. "Truman."

A weak groan came in response.

"Truman." Bolan elbowed him again. "We have to get up."

Hitihiti's immense mass shuddered. A different kind of groan ripped from his throat. The Tongan rolled his bulk onto his side as he began to spew up half of the Solomon Sea.

He'd live.

Bolan let him finish heaving and then hauled him to his

knees by the collar of his life vest. "Come on. We've got to get into the trees."

"Right…trees." Hitihiti shucked off of the vest and cast it aside.

"Truman." Bolan frowned at the big man. "Don't leave that on the beach."

"What?" Hitihiti reeled under Bolan's gaze. "Right, no traces."

Bolan caught the man as he began to buckle. He draped one of the Tongan's arms across his shoulder, and the two men staggered into the trees.

Amsterdam

THE MEN WERE professional killers.

Rutgers regarded his team with a great sense of pride. He had not cared for the way Craig had taken over his company. He had not cared for it at all.

Craig had been very blunt about the matter. He didn't give a shit if Rutgers liked it or not. Craig needed a job done. The swift, successful execution of that job would result in the biggest payday of Rutgers's life and the return of the Executive Options company to him, as sole shareholder. There was another enticing perk to the job. Rutgers had a blank check as far as expenses went. He also had free rein to conduct the campaign any way he wanted. All Craig cared about was results. Swift results. He did not want a political uprising. He wanted the situation settled before the United Nations could get involved.

An unlimited expense account, no outside interference and no rules of engagement were a very rare mixture of blessings in the merc business.

Rutgers spent a moment looking through the window of the airport bar.

Eight very dangerous men lounged in a booth drinking lager and eyeing the hostesses. Most people in the bar felt vaguely intimidated by the table of red-eyed, jet-lagged men but could not have explained why. Rutgers could have told them. The citizens had every right to be nervous.

Thom Jensen was a master sniper. Both Piet Dunkan and Tymon Corboline were expert trackers, who had learned the trade of tracking and killing the most elusive of prey alongside bushmen in the Kalahari Desert. Valdemar Solomon's dark skin reflected his mixed Indian, African and Boer origins, and if there was a more dangerous knife fighter on Earth Rutgers had never heard of him. Steppan Gotwald was the team leader and a veteran of battles on three continents, including action on the neighboring isle of Bougainville. Pol Thomas was an artist with demolitions who painted abstracts in plastic explosive. Behind the lazy smile of pilot David Kiins lurked a brutal expert in psychological warfare. Rutgers smiled as he regarded the final member of the team. Bryce Delvoix was simply the dirtiest bastard Rutgers had ever known. All were former South African Defense Force Reconnaissance commandos. Every one of them had made sergeant. Each had led men into battle, and won. They were the most trusted and able men on the Executive Options roster.

Rutgers had thought long and hard about the situation on Pa'ahnui and what the mission required to succeed.

Rutgers did not need a lot of men. The island was already festering with Russian thugs and Menzies security agents, with the promise of more already on the way. All the cannon fodder needed to overwhelm the local resistance was already in place. A cursory review of the late Schutte Kliivland's reports revealed the one thing lacking for total success.

Leaders.

The Russians needed to have their asses kicked back in

line. They needed to start acting like soldiers rather than brigands.

What was needed was discipline.

Rutgers smiled as he stepped into the bar and greeted his motivational team.

TREVOR BURDICK KNEW he was being tracked.

He crouched in the undergrowth. A wave had ripped him and Hitihiti apart before he could lash their vests together. Burdick felt bad about that. He had spent immense amounts of energy thrashing around in the chop trying to find the unconscious Tongan before being forced to concede to the surf and concentrate on his own survival.

The big ex-Marine had woken up facedown in the sand before dawn. He was glad to be alive. Burdick had waited on the beach while the last stars faded and the sky turned purple, hoping to find Bolan or Hitihiti, but the sound of a helicopter had driven him inland under the jungle canopy. He had stuffed his life vest in a hollow log. It was about then that he had heard the popping of gunfire in the distance. The big ex-Marine found fresh boot tracks and followed them inland.

At about eight in the morning, the tracks had doubled back and disappeared. Burdick was very aware that now he was being hunted.

He didn't have a gun. He'd escaped the demise of the *Bread and Butter* with little more than his shirt, shorts and Truman Hitihiti's unconscious body, and he had lost the Tongan. Sometime in his night of being hurled about upon the ocean, his folding knife had come unclipped from his pocket and gone down into the brine. Burdick paused. He glanced around his immediate surroundings and considered his options in armament.

Burdick took the only option available. He uprooted a two-inch-diameter sapling from the jungle floor and quietly stripped it of its branches with a rock. His Irish ancestors would have been proud of the shillelagh he'd produced. Red smeared his face, arms and legs with mud, and began to creep through the undergrowth once more with a catlike grace that belied his bulk. He held the sapling ready for a skull-smashing blow with the root-ball.

He was Force Recon, and the shithead tracking him was in a lot of trouble.

Burdick froze at the metallic sound of a weapon's safety flicking off.

"G'day." The voice spoke from the boulders behind him. "Lose the kindling."

Burdick dropped the sapling.

"Put up your hands, slowly. Turn around"

Burdick did as he was told. He blinked in surprise as he found himself staring at a very weathered-looking old man in stained khakis and floppy hat. Some kind of blue, brindle-furred dingo-looking mutt was silently baring its teeth. The man was pointing what looked like a wad of turn of the century plumbing parts at him.

"Wow." Red smiled out of the mud covering his face. "Owen gun. That's a grand old piece you got there, Dad."

"That's 'Inspector' to you, mate." The man looked at Red in surprise. "A Yank, then?"

"Red, white and blue."

The inspector chewed this over. "You're not with the Russians, are you?"

"Inspector, I'm with the United States Marines."

The Australian eyed the sapling and the mass of its root-ball. "Trees are U.S. kit these days, then?"

"Oh, well." Red shrugged. "My boat sank last night. I washed up about three hours ago. I'm looking for two of my friends who might have survived."

The man suddenly looked hopeful. "More Marines, then?"

"No, but a fellow American."

"So who's your third?"

"A Polynesian. We were on his boat."

"Polynesian?" The inspector blinked. "Truman Hitihiti, is it?"

Red grinned. "That's the man!"

"Wrong answer." The inspector raised the gun to his shoulder. "You hang out with the wrong sort, mate. That can get you into trouble around here."

The dog caught its master's mood and growled.

"Jesus! He was just our transportation!" Red verbally backpedaled. "And he was the only asshole in the Solomon Islands willing to make a run at the blockade."

The inspector seemed to accept that at face value, but the muzzle of the Owen never wavered. "What do you want on Pa'ahnui, then?"

"My friend and I, we're…" Red decided the truth was his best option, however lame it sounded. "Well, we're looking for a friend of ours. He's gone missing."

"A friend gone missing here on the island? What friend?"

"A black guy."

The old man smiled dryly. "Well, just about everyone on this island is black, mate."

"Yeah, but my friend is an American. Named Calvin. He's with the resistance. You seen him?"

"No." The inspector lowered his weapon as he digested this, but only slightly. "But I might have heard a rumor of him."

"Yeah, well, I'm looking for him. I'd appreciate it if you could point me in the direction of the good guys."

"Well, that's easy." The old man's eyes traveled toward the mist shrouded peaks. "The direction is up, but they'll find you before you find them, and they're killing any white man they see."

"Well, that sucks." Red was fresh out of ideas.

"Listen, I think you and I need to yabber a bit more, but not here." The inspector came to a decision. "You look like you could use some tucker. Join me in my cave?"

Trevor Burdick didn't know what tucker was, but he was pretty sure he could use some. "Sure, yeah, fine. I'd, uh, love to see your cave and…tucker."

"Right, you first, then." The inspector pointed his muzzle inland. "And leave the tree."

Church of England

WHISTLES AND CATCALLS met the woman as she strode from the helicopter pad. They were weary and desultory and died off when two massive men in tropical weight blue suits followed her. The two black mastiffs drew even more respectful stares. The woman looked around at the situation, and she was not pleased.

If Pa'ahnui had a capital, Church of England was it. Originally a coastal fishing village, it was where the English missionaries had built their church. The trading post the missionaries had set up to help support themselves was an outbuilding of the little church. Natives throughout the island traditionally came to the church on Sundays, initially to hear the sermon. They also came to trade and take part in what swiftly became all-day swap meets, followed by a buffet. If anyone had a specific grievance, the inspector always attended services and was there to mediate.

The church became a focal point, and Church of England became the de facto name of a village that had never before bothered with one.

The woman surveyed the carnage.

All the miners and Menzies employees other than the security agents had been evacuated. With their commander dead and an open playing field, the Russians had gone on a rampage.

Half of the native huts on the outskirts of the one-lane town were burning. The Menzies Company housing on the east side of the town, which was provided for relocated natives had been looted, as well. There was hardly a building standing that did not have bullet holes in its front. The church was partially burnt. The crucifix had been ripped off the wall inside and planted in the garden outside.

She had seen the smoke plumes rising into the dawn as she landed, and she could only imagine what had gone on in the interior.

None of this bothered the woman in the slightest.

What disgusted her was the readily apparent lack of discipline. The few Russians on the street were staggering drunk. Tottering about and blinking into the rising sun like the morning after Armageddon. The few light support weapons she saw were mounted on jeeps that were parked here and there and were unmanned. There were no emplaced weapons on the perimeter.

There was no perimeter.

With any luck the natives were still shell-shocked, shuddering and hiding in the trees, reeling from the Russians' drunken rampage, but that would not last. The native population of the island was estimated to be around ten thousand, though that had probably been somewhat reduced in the past forty-eight hours. The fact was, Church of England and the whole Menzies mining operation could fall at any moment.

All it would take would be just one enraged charge out of the jungle by a thousand spear- and machete-armed natives hell-bent on revenge.

Ilya Gaz sat oblivious in the middle of the still smoldering town square. The Russian was stripped to the waist and reclining like the heir apparent in a commandeered reclining chair. He held a brown, mostly empty bottle of native palm wine in one hand and a Czech CZ-75 machine pistol in the other. Gaz was a remarkably ugly man in a myriad of unfortunate ways. His wiry, sunburned physique was covered with tattoos, many of them marred by scar tissue. He sat, the debauched king of a hell on Earth of his own creation. His laconic smile revealed gold from numerous replaced teeth. He smiled now as the woman approached him. Her nose wrinkled as she closed. Gaz stank with a heady mixture of sweat, sex, gun smoke, liquor and marijuana. The Russian's fly was undone, and his red eyes traveled up and down her body lasciviously.

"You…" He pointed a bloody finger and sat up with renewed interest. "You are the boss's bitch. I'm the boss here, you—"

Ilya's front teeth flew out of his head as he flew backward over the chair. The woman wiped the blood from her boot in the sand.

Gaz rose spitting blood and obscenities.

He ceased his swearing as the selector lever of the woman's Drotik machine pistol flicked to the 3-round burst setting. The muzzle was pointed directly between his eyes. The laser sight beneath it lit up and painted a red dot where his eyebrows met.

The woman spoke in Russian. "Ilya, you're a mess."

Gaz's hands clenched into fists. He glared at a nearby house. Two of his men who had been lounging on the veranda smoking hemp were now on their feet watching the altercation. Gaz snarled at his men for backup. "Tyoma! Marik!"

The men fingered their automatic carbines nervously as

they examined the woman, her bodyguards, her dogs and the bullet-riddled helicopter she had just flown in on. Tyoma and Marik did the math and sat down.

"Useless pricks." Gaz spit out another tooth and resumed staring down the machine pistol's muzzle defiantly. "Fuck you. Bitch."

The woman smiled. "Ilya, you have reinforcements coming, and you have a new commander."

"Reinforcements?" Despite the weapon pointed at his head, Gaz ogled the woman's athletic thighs. He waved his arms around at the smoking ruins of the village. "Look at this place! It is fucking pacified. I tell you, anything that moves gets shot or fucked." Ilya grinned impishly. "So nothing moves."

"Yes. I see that." The woman's eyes traveled to the volcanic peaks above them. "And up there?"

Ilya lost his grin. "Fuck them."

"Like I said, you have reinforcements coming and a new commander."

Gaz rolled his eyes. "Another South African faggot?"

"Oh, yes." The woman smiled benevolently. "Rutgers. You've heard of him?"

Ilya's face went blank. "Executive Options Rutgers?"

"Right."

"He's coming here?"

"Yes, indeed."

Despite the haze of liquor and drugs, wheels turned in Ilya's mind. "Fuck."

"Exactly." The woman gazed around at the destruction of the village. "And what do you think he's going to do when he sees…this?"

Ilya had no prepared response.

"He is going to make examples out of people, that's what he's going to do," she said.

Gaz blanched.

"Commander Rutgers is authorized to take any action he sees fit. He is in complete command. If he decides to negotiate with the rebels, your head is one of the bargaining chips."

Gaz fell back on his strengths. "Fuck you. Bitch."

"Mmm." The woman nodded. "Listen, Ilya. I don't give a shit about you, but I am going to give you a piece of advice." She made a graceful, panoramic gesture that encompassed the entire situation. "Clean up this shit. Clean up your men."

Gaz went sullen again.

"Try this—pretend you're back in Chechnya. The rebels are massing. Set up a perimeter. Make this place look like there are soldiers keeping order, and when Rutgers shows up, obey orders." The woman smiled meaningfully. "Better than that, make yourself useful."

Gaz hawked, spit more blood and nodded. "I'll set up a perimeter."

"Good, and I'll give you two missions until Rutgers gets here."

"Missions?" Gaz raised a scarred eyebrow.

"Yes. The rebels have been trying to sneak mercs and weapons onto the island."

"Like the black American." Ilya's face grew even more unpleasant. "I owe him."

"Yes, you do. We sank a boat last night loaded with weapons and mercenary advisers headed for the rebels. There may be more. I want you to send out men, keep your guns down, your dicks in your pants and offer rewards for information."

"Okay…" Gaz glanced around. "But a lot of my men are out—" he searched for a diplomatic word "—doing…reconnaissance."

The woman snorted in disgust. "Get your men back in. Get them organized, and get them back out working. And one more thing. We have become aware of the fact that there is a reporter on the island."

"A reporter?" Gaz shook his head. "What the fuck are you talking about?"

"We don't know how she got here, but she is trying to meet with the rebels and get their story out to the media. Find her, and bring her to Rutgers, alive. Offer ten thousand U.S. dollars to anyone who can provide information on where she is. Her name is Juliet Thomas. She's redheaded, American. Find her, or get information on where she is. If she's in the highlands already, find out which village. Rutgers will do the rest."

Gaz nodded. "Okay, information. I can get that."

"Good." The woman snapped her fingers and chopped her hand through the air. "Hitler! Stalin!"

The mastiffs lunged forward and knocked Gaz back into his chair. The gigantic dogs stood over him, paws on his chest, exposing their fangs and drooling in his face. Their blue eyes stared into his with the gift of emptiness. They were machines. They would kill anything at the whim of their master.

Or mistress.

"Ilya." The woman turned away and began walking back to the helicopter. "You screw this up, and I will feed you to these dogs."

The woman snapped her fingers, and the dogs heeled behind her.

Gaz sat for a moment shaking with an adrenaline rush and drooling blood. He waited until his visitors were back in their aircraft before he shot to his feet roaring with rage. "Tyoma! Marik! Get your limp pricks over here!" Gaz scooped up his pistol and kicked away the spilled bottle of palm wine. "I have a job for you!"

6

The Russians were coming.

Bolan measured the tonnage. Truman was still green around the gills, but his eyes were hard. "You ready for this?"

"Ready for this?" Hitihiti eyed Bolan's weapon incredulously. "With that?"

Bolan had ripped the tongue from one of his boots and cut it into a two-inch oblong. He had punched two holes into each side and firmly knotted his bootlaces into them, then knotted the ends of each pair of laces. Bolan folded a smooth stone about the size of a hen's egg into the tongue and took the two feet of bootlaces into his right hand. He gave the contraption a few practice rotations. In an eye blink, the makeshift sling was a humming blur.

With his left hand, Bolan pointed at a tree fifty feet away and released. Bark flew like shrapnel, and outraged bats exploded out of the boughs above. A two-inch crater in the trunk oozed sap where it had been struck.

"Okay," Truman conceded. "I'm down with it." He grinned. "David and Goliath are on the same team this time, brah."

Bolan pulled another stone from his pocket and reloaded the sling. "You want a club or a rock or something?"

"Naw." Hitihiti held up callused hands the size of catchers' mitts. "God gave me a gift."

The two men squatted in the undergrowth by the side of the road and waited. The road was less than a year old and cut through the jungle like a knife of asphalt. It was not yet noon, and heat mirages already simmered off its black surface. Bolan cocked his head. "A jeep is coming this way, from the interior, and we need their guns."

"Right."

"You know the drill?"

"You suck 'em in. I smash 'em down." Hitihiti raised his bulk and began to move back into the trees. "I'll be waiting."

Bolan crouched and watched the road. A beige jeep appeared in the distance. It was jacked up on huge off-road tires. A Russian PK medium machine gun was mounted on a post in the back bed, but it was not being manned. Of more immediate importance was the fact that the front windshield had been lowered and an RPK light machine gun was mounted in front of the passenger's seat. There were four men, two in front, two lounging in back.

Four was a lot.

Bolan would have to get close. He had to take out the driver and not get cut to ribbons in the process. Deception was his best bet.

The Executioner stepped into the middle of the road.

The men in the jeep looked up, but what they saw was a white man in khaki shorts, boots and a T-shirt stepping out of the jungle.

For a few crucial seconds, the Russians saw one of their own.

Bolan smiled and waved.

The front machine gunner raised a bottle of beer and waved back as the jeep drove within killing range.

The Russians had one second to look at Bolan quizzically as he wound up and let fly. The driver's head snapped back like he had been shot and then rubbernecked forward.

The jeep lurched and swerved as the dead man fell against the wheel.

Bolan dived into the underbrush.

Behind him, he heard the jeep crash into a tree but not nearly hard enough. Within seconds, bullets were ripping into the jungle above his head. Bolan belly crawled deeper into the trees. Men shouted in Russian. More bullets tore into the jungle, followed by the sound of men crashing through the brush.

Bolan rose and ran. He loaded a rock into his sling and turned. The weapon blurred at his side like a propeller.

A Russian came bounding through the trees, but there was too much intervening jungle to take the shot. The Russian's head jerked up as he caught sight of Bolan, and he charged with his carbine snarling on full-auto. The burst cut short as Truman Hitihiti erupted out of the shrubbery and clotheslined the Russian across the clavicles. The Russian pinwheeled around the Tongan's fire-hose-sized arm, and the back of his head bounced brutally against the jungle floor.

Hitihiti raised his hand high over his head. He curled his hand into a fist and brought it crashing down like a hammer onto the left side of his fallen opponent's chest. The Russian's arms and legs spasmed once, then were still. Hitihiti scooped up the man's carbine and began tearing at the Russian's web gear.

Tracers drew smoking lines through the trees.

"Shit!" Hitihiti threw himself flat as the long sustained snarl of a machine gun chopped through the trees at chest level. He fired a burst back and rolled as answering fire ripped across the ground he had just occupied and tore chunks out of the dead Russian's corpse. Truman blasted off another burst and plunged through the trees.

Bolan sank down. The enemy was no longer advancing.

Hitihiti crawled to their regrouping point and sat against a rock wheezing. "I got a gun, brah."

"I noticed." Bolan glanced at the AKSU. It looked like a toy in the Tongan's hands. "How many rounds left?"

Truman clicked out the magazine, glanced at it and shoved it back. "Five, maybe six?"

"Yeah," Bolan sighed wearily. "Set it on semiauto."

"What you think they're doing?" Truman flicked his selector to semiauto and peered through the cover. "Why don't they come and get us?"

"They're waiting for backup." Bolan glanced up. There was a great deal of shouting out by the road. Far more than two men could make. "And it sounds like it's shown up."

The sound of men thrashing their way through the jungle came increasingly near.

"What you wanna do, brah?"

"Why don't you give me the rifle?"

The Tongan frowned. "What am I supposed to do then?"

"I don't know." Bolan shrugged. "Run?"

"Really?" Hitihiti stared in disbelief. "You mean that?"

"Get out of here, Truman. You didn't sign up for this." Bolan reached into his pocket and pulled out the thick, sea-stained clip of currencies. "Get to the coast, find a fishing village. There should be enough there to get a boat, get yourself safely arrested by the Papuan naval blockade and bribe you way back to the Solomons."

Hitihiti took the cash. His eyes stared long and hard at warrior before him. "That's a big gift. Real big."

"Just give me the gun and go."

The Tongan handed over the carbine, nodded once and disappeared into the jungle. Bolan checked the magazine for himself. He had six bullets in the clip and one in the chamber. He adjusted his sights for fifty yards and waited.

He did not have to wait long.

The Russians were coming in an arrow-shaped patrol. There were at least six he could see, with one of the machine gunners hanging back. Bolan suspected there was an equal number farther out that he couldn't see.

Bolan began to flank them. He moved eastward a few dozen feet. He needed to get across the road so he could escape into the interior. In a few seconds, the leading element of the combat patrol would find their traces. On cue, a Russian walked into the tiny clearing and saw footprints in the mud. He blew a whistle, and more men began to converge.

The whistle's shriek was cut short as Bolan shot the man through the thigh. The Executioner faded farther around in a large circle as two more men burst into the clearing and began firing long bursts at nothing in particular while the man on the ground screamed.

Bolan picked his line through the trees and shot each man through the leg. The Russians fell howling. One had the presence of mind to note Bolan's muzzle-blast and fire off a long burst in his direction. Two more Russians bounded into view and continued firing. Bolan was forced to retreat.

He had four bullets left.

Bolan doubled back, swinging toward the road, but the enemy skirmish line had already closed that avenue. Russian battle whistles were shrilling everywhere. It sounded like backup had arrived in platoon strength. They were going to drive him toward the beach and out into the open.

An RPG-7 grenade sizzled through the jungle and smashed short of Bolan as it hit a tree. The soldier turned and shot the rocketeer in the face. He was down to three rounds, and the whistles were converging. It was no longer a hunt.

It was a chase.

Bolan ran.

The Executioner had spent the night bobbing in the ocean and hadn't had anything to eat or drink in twenty hours. He could feel his legs beginning to fail him. He picked a path through the trees and sprinted for all he was worth. The lactic acid of exhaustion turned his muscles rubbery and his sprint into an enfeebled trot. He burst into a clearing and tracers sought him.

Bolan turned as the Russians burst into the clearing after him.

Truman Hitihiti suddenly rose from behind a rock. He held a revolver in his hand. The pistol barked twice as he shot the first two Russians into the clearing. More Russians spilled into the open. Trevor Burdick leaned from around a tree on their flank. The sawed-off shotgun he held thudded twice, and two more Russians fell with ruptured chests. Bolan fired two rounds back the way he had come, and another Russian went down.

Burdick waved Bolan on, and he bolted for the other side of the clearing.

Two more Russians broke out, blowing their whistles and spraying their weapons.

A man with a submachine gun on their right flank burned them to the ground.

Bolan dived into jungle. Hitihiti and Burdick had already circled around, and the soldier followed Red as the big man plunged through the trees with an apparent destination in mind.

The Russians had stopped.

The clearing was a killing zone, and they had lost too many men to it. They would be regrouping. If they were smart, they were calling in helicopters. Bolan stumbled after Red. They came to another clearing where an elderly gentleman with a submachine gun sat on a rock wheezing from his run. He looked up and waved as he saw Burdick. It took him several long moments to catch his breath.

"G'day."

Bolan took a few moments of his own. He took in the man's gun, accent and age. "Afternoon, Inspector. Thanks for the rescue. I owe you."

"Well, I ran into Red this morning. We were having a bit of powwow when we heard your ruckus. Ran into Truman." The Australian shrugged. "No worries."

Bolan examined the jungle surrounding them. "You have a hide close by?"

"Got a cave." The old man pushed himself to his feet and mopped his brow. "But the Russkies'll turn it up soon enough, now I reckon. Best move on a stretch."

Bolan looked toward the mountains. "You'll take us to meet the rebels?"

"Get you close. Whether we see them or not is up to them. I gotta get a few things first. You manage to get any guns or ammo off the Russians?"

Bolan held up the carbine. "One bullet left."

"Yeah, we're all a bit thin." He took in Bolan's condition. "You eaten?"

"Not lately."

"Well," the inspector nodded. "Let's get some fuel into you before we go meet the locals."

"I'd appreciate that."

"Yeah, well. Best to tuck in now." The Australian smiled. "With the highlanders on the warpath you can never be quite sure if you'll be staying for dinner or if you're the main course."

Church of England

Things were looking a lot better. The little port town wouldn't pass a United Nations Human Rights Tribunal investigation, but with luck it might just pass inspection by Rutgers and his commandos. It had taken a few busted heads and the ambush out by the road, but Ilya Gaz had motivated his men. There were roadblocks on either side of town, and the inland huts ringing the outside of the village had been bulldozed. The trees had been cleared to create a three-hundred-foot dead zone between the village and the jungle. A seven-foot trench had been dug and filled with sharpened bamboo stakes. Coils of gleaming razor wire were strung along the top. Three machine gun nests had been sandbagged along the defensive line with interlocking fields of fire. The top of the church steeple was gone, and the bell ripped out. Planks had been hammered into place to make a larger, sandbagged platform. A light machine gunner and a sniper with night-vision equipment were on watch day and night.

Gaz made a call. "We've made contact with those mercenaries you were talking about."

The woman's voice sounded bemused. "Did you kill them?"

"No."

"And how many of your weapons did they manage to requisition?"

Gaz grunted. "One carbine."

"Really. Well, that's something, anyway. Did you confirm their identities?"

Gaz glanced down at the sketches he'd been faxed. "According to my men, one of them was definitely Hitihiti. The other two they are not sure of, but the resemblance is close enough that I am assuming these are the men you described."

"Did you find the reporter?"

"No, but I have circulated the news about a reward for her and for information about the American mercenaries."

"Good, what else do you have to report?"

"The inspector is missing."

The woman mentally checked her notes. "The Australian?"

"Yes, that one."

"He's an old man. Retired."

"We ransacked his house. He had a shotgun and a revolver. We also found a crate for a submachine gun. He and the weapons are missing."

"Interesting. I'll do some research on him."

Gaz came to the nagging question. "So, Rutgers—he is really coming?"

"He's gathering his men. They should be leaving tonight. It will take them a few hops to get there, but you may expect him soon."

Gaz looked out from the shattered window of the Menzies corporate office on the island and examined his field fortifications. His men had been sober for twenty-four hours. The three who hadn't bothered had been beaten and thrown down a cellar until they were.

The woman knew Gaz was worried about Rutgers's arrival. Gaz had good reason to be nervous. Stephen Craig was also arriving, and if Gaz had even the slightest clue, he would have jumped in the volcano already and spared himself the agony to come. "Don't be nervous. My sources say you've cleaned up the place pretty well," she said.

Gaz cursed under his breath. "Her sources." That meant one or more of his men. "When are you coming back?" he asked.

"Not for a few days. I have some business to take care of."

"I don't need Rutgers," Gaz insisted. "I need heavy weapons. I need gunships."

Gaz couldn't see the curl of the woman's lips on the other end of the phone. "You've got more coming than you can imagine."

THEY WERE SURROUNDED.

The Pa'ahnui highlands were a very cold wet place in the morning. In their battered shape, it had taken Bolan's team a day to sneak across the road cut through one of the inland valleys and begin the steep climb up the central mountain. They were literally walking inside a cloud.

A rain cloud.

Inspector Filmoore stopped to light a cigarette and frowned at the soggy state of his matchbook. He perked an eyebrow at Bolan. "Striker?"

Bolan struck a waterproof match and gave the inspector a light. "Yeah?"

The inspector nodded gratefully and muttered around his cigarette, "We're surrounded."

"I know." Bolan did not glance around. Red and Hitihiti had been watching their feet and gasping for the last hour of the climb and were blissfully unaware. "They've been shadowing us for the last half hour," Bolan said.

"Well I'll be stuffed." The inspector eyed Bolan respectfully. "I only picked up on them five minutes ago."

"I smelled the hemp they've been burning this morning."

"Well, the highlanders like to bake a bit." Filmoore smiled wearily. "Let's hope it makes them reasonable."

"Let's hope it doesn't give them the goddamn munchies," Red said, gasping. "I've heard the rumors about these guys. What's happening?"

Bolan kept the muzzle of his carbine pointed at the ground and nodded ahead. "That."

A man materialized out of the mist like a ghost. He was dark skinned with a lean, ropey physique. He was wearing a sarong, a Che Guevara T-shirt with the sleeves cut off and a beret with a handmade revolutionary red star sewn into it. His dark hair fell in waves to his shoulders. A Russian Makarov pistol had been thrust in the waist of his sarong. A war club shaped like an elongated table tennis paddle hung from his wrist by a leather thong. It appeared to be made out of solid jade. The edges glittered with glasslike sharpness.

The highlander nodded at Filmoore and spoke English with an unidentifiable accent. "Hey, Inspector."

The inspector tipped his hat. "G'day, Sho."

The man considered the party before him. "Told you, Inspector. You got no authority in the highlands."

"Not asking for any, Sho. Nor enforcin'."

"Well, that's good." The highlander looked at each man again. "You longtime island man, Inspector. I know you. I think maybe you okay." He gestured broadly at the inspector's companions. "But I told you last time you come up here. I kill any white man mainlander who come up into highlands now."

Hitihiti thrust out his jaw. "Who you calling white man, brah?"

"I know you, Truman." The highlander smiled with little warmth. "Know you an asshole."

The Polynesian spat at the Melanesian's feet. "Fuck you."

All around them the underbrush rustled. Bolan and his companions were instantly surrounded by forty men, painted for war and armed with stone-tipped spears. A scattering of them had Russian automatic carbines.

"No, Truman." The highlander pursed his lips and shook his head sadly. "Fuck you."

"Yeah, well, who are you calling a mainlander?" All eyes turned as Burdick dropped his shotgun to the ground and jammed a thumb against his chest in disgust. "I'm Irish! An island boy! You got that? The white man's been keeping my people down for a thousand years." He jerked his head at Bolan. "You want to kill the oppressor? Kill the American over here."

The highlander blinked at the massive Marine.

"Thanks, Red," Bolan said as he measured the man before him. "You're Hose Sh'sho?"

"No." The man's face was a stone mask. "Hose was my father. He's dead. Russians killed him. I'm his son. Bawamuni Sh'sho."

"I heard your father was a good soldier. I'm sorry. Calvin respected him."

"No sorry." Sh'sho shook his head. "He died a warrior. He's with the ancestors now. Not living like some whore or houseboy down mountain."

"I respect that." The Executioner took a step forward. "I'm a friend of Calvin James."

The highlander looked Bolan up and down. "You the Strikerman he told me about?"

"That would be me."

"You know, word out. You got ten thousand dollars on your head."

Bolan shrugged. "I've had more."

"Ten thousand U.S." Sho slapped his thigh. "That buys a lot of rifles, GI."

"The only man running rifles to Pa'ahnui is Truman, and

his boat is at the bottom of the Solomon Sea." Bolan smiled. "And you really don't want to piss off Calvin James by selling one of his friends to the enemy."

"True." The highlander pushed his beret back on his head and looked up into the morning sun as it began to break up the mist.

The ring of natives seemed to relax as Bolan and Sho spoke. Sho seemed happier, too. "So. You come here to help us?"

"No." Bolan locked his gaze with the highlander. "I came here to bring Calvin back."

The man stared at Bolan blankly.

The hedge of spear points surrounding Bolan's party rose again.

"Calvin came here because of your father. They were like brothers. Calvin is like my brother. He's not going to die for nothing. Not until I talk with him."

"We're nothing?" The highlander's war club was in his hand.

"No, but barring a miracle, you're a lost cause."

"Lost cause?"

"You can't win."

The highlander flinched.

Bolan looked at the spears surrounding him. "This is your greeting party. The one you send out to meet guests invited or otherwise. This is your Sunday best, and I count seven rifles. Spears and war clubs aren't going to cut it in this war, Sho, and you know it. I need to speak to Calvin, and I need to speak to your elders. We need to start thinking about what can be salvaged out of this situation."

"You know? You don't bring good news, Strikerman." The highlander stared into the mist. "But Father always trusted Calvin James. Calvin James say you okay. Old men want to talk to you."

He let the war club hang freely. "We should at least let Calvin James speak with you before we eat you."

Philippines

EDGAR GABRIELLO WAS a genuine pirate. He had been born small and homely. This had led to an adolescent obsession with weightlifting and bladed weapons. Payback on those who had tormented him throughout his youth had been swift. The resulting price on his head had forced him into exile from his native island of Palawan. This chain of events had led him to a lucrative and personally rewarding career of raping, pillaging and hijacking from the Andaman to the Coral Sea.

The Filipino pirate was not a brilliant man, but he had a highly developed sense of cunning. He had learned a few things in his career about survival. Most of his mind was blearily focused on his desire to conquer the white woman before him to the cheers of his men.

Instead, he leaned back into the shining teak and stainless-steel throne of his custom fishing chair. His hand rested on the rosewood grips of his Smith & Wesson Model 29 .44 Magnum revolver. His instincts told him that the woman was not to be fucked with.

"What do you want, bitch?" he asked, testing the boundaries.

The woman raised an eyebrow in challenge. "What do you want, Edgar?"

"I wanna fuck you." He grinned like an orangutan as his men roared in approval.

"Well…" the woman conceded modestly, "I can see how you might say that. But there are other things you want, aren't there?"

The pirate's eyes narrowed behind his thick glasses. "What are you talking about?"

"Oh, I don't know. Guns? Gold? Jade? Cash? Free rein to

loot and pillage an entire island. Maybe…" The woman waved a graceful hand in suggestion. "Truman Hitihiti's head?"

"Truman Hitihiti!" The pirate's face split into an ugly snarl. "Fuck him!"

"Yes, I understand the two of you have had some run-ins. As I understand it, you've always gotten the short end of it."

"Fuck Truman!" He stabbed a finger at the woman. "Fuck you!"

"You know, Edgar? I happen to know where Truman is, and I'll tell you something for nothing—he's in a bad way." The woman's smile turned genuine as she captured Gabriello's undivided attention. "I'd describe his current situation as genuinely vulnerable."

The pirate looked alert.

"You've heard of Pa'ahnui?" the woman asked.

"I hear there's a revolution on it."

"That's right."

"Revolutions no good." He chewed his lip. "No money in them."

"There is in this one, and there's Truman."

The pirate squinted suspiciously. "Truman helping the rebels?"

"So it seems."

"Fucking Truman." Gabriello shook his head. "He always talk about his personal code, code of the warrior. Polynesian shit! Fuck him! Fuck his code! Truman an errand boy! Taking shit from here to there! Me?" Gabriello drew the snake-curved blade of his Damascus steel kris and shoved it high into the air. "I just take shit! Any shit I want!"

The pirates about him drew knives and *parangs* and waved them as they shouted in agreement.

"Well, I'm looking for a man who might just take Truman

Hitihiti's head." The woman looked around at the pirates. Most carried an automatic rifle or submachine gun. All were festooned with pistols and bladed weapons of every description. "I need you and about a hundred of your men on Pa'ahnui, immediately."

"How do we get past the blockade?" Gabriello asked.

"The back door will be open. It's been arranged."

8

"It's about time."

Calvin James surveyed Bolan's state of affairs. "Don't suppose you brought any guns?"

"Had them for you, but we got sunk." Bolan took a seat and Sh'sho sat next to him. Bolan turned to Burdick and Hitihiti. "Give me a few minutes with the man."

Bolan spoke low as the two giants shambled off. "Hal sent me. The NSA picked up your broadcast, and my numbers ran up flags at the Farm. They put two and two together and figured out what you're up to here on Pa'ahnui. I think you've pissed some people off in the State Department. Rogue U.S. agent assisting Communist revolution and all that."

"The people here aren't communists."

Bolan looked at the tiny village. "Well, you and I know that, but that's the official line the Australian and Papuan governments are holding, and so is Menzies mining and the Craig Consortium, and to tell you the truth Cal? No one gives a damn. I read the surveyor's reports. You're clogging up hundreds of millions of dollars in profits, and that's what's doing all the talking."

It was nothing James didn't already know. He closed his eyes for a moment. "So Hal sent you to bring me back?" he asked.

"The President told Hal to tell me to extract you."

James opened his eyes with amused wariness. "Extract?"

"Those were the words used." Bolan smiled. "I told Hal I'd ask you politely."

"Well, that's decent of you."

"Calvin."

"Yes, Striker?"

"Please come home."

James closed his eyes again. "No."

"Now that we've got that out of the way, how's the Pa'ahnui People's Revolution?"

"It sucks." James scowled and looked at Bolan. "The coastal and valley villages have all capitulated or been terrorized into submission. Here in the highlands, we've sent a couple of Menzies security probes home with bloody noses, but we've heard all about the Russians they brought in. We saw the fires and could hear the gunshots and screaming down below the other night. Sounds like they pulled a Four Horsemen of the Apocalypse on the lowlanders."

"That's about the size of it. According to the inspector, it got real ugly down there."

"Yeah, and it's gonna get real ugly up here, too," James said. "Shit, it's only a matter of time before they come up here in strength, and you can count our guns on two hands. We've seen that helicopter flying around. I'm surprised they haven't hit us with gunships yet."

"We got sunk forty-eight hours ago by that helicopter. They made rocket runs on us. We damaged it some, but it's still airworthy." Bolan glanced at the sky. "Gunships will be coming, Cal."

James stared into the blue sky and said nothing.

"So what are you going to do? Throw spears at them?" Bolan asked.

"I don't know. Try to ambush some patrols, take out some sentries, take their guns. Infiltrate." James exposed his teeth. "The usual Communist revolutionary guerrilla bullshit."

"That's not going to work. This island is just too small. They'll turn Church of England into a fortress if they're smart. Then with their perimeter secure, they'll bring in gunships, and come in force. You can only hide up here so long, and then they're going to come up in force and slaughter you."

That scenario had been clearly weighing on the ex-Navy SEAL's mind.

Bolan drew a line in the dirt with a stick. "You're going to have to attack, now." He looked at Sh'sho. "Or you're going to have to surrender. Those are your only options."

"We have eyes on Church of England. You're right. They make fort. Dig ditches. Make tower. Guns. Lots and lots of guns."

James put his chin in his palms. "We need guns."

"Red brought you guns, rockets and recoilless rifles, but they all went down with the ship. You're going to have to get the entire island to rise up, Cal. It's the only way. We're talking a real night of the long knives. The entire island has to swarm C of E in one overwhelming mass, and you had better expect to take hundreds, maybe thousands of casualties."

"There's barely ten thousand people on this island." James shook his head slowly. "You're talking about annihilating most of the adult male population."

"Without guns, that's what its going to come down to." Again Bolan turned to Sh'sho. "I seriously suggest that you consider surrender."

"To become a houseboy?" She looked around and pointed at a woman nearby. "See my sister be a miner's whore? No. Better to fight. Better to die like father."

Bolan could see where Sh'sho was going. "Calvin, with a

radio, maybe, we could arrange something, get someone to smuggle some weapons here, but even that would take time."

"You don't think I know that?"

Sh'sho lit a pipe and glared into the forest. "Need guns."

"I know guns."

The men looked up.

Sh'sho's sister had approached them, and she shrugged at what was glaringly obvious to her. "Have to be guns."

"That crazy talk Si-Se!" Sh'sho's eyes bugged as he discerned what she was talking about. "You know forbidden!"

A rapid-fire argument in the local language erupted.

Sho shook his head repeatedly. "Bad…bad…bad," he said.

"Have to be guns," his sister insisted. She lifted her chin defiantly and smiled at Bolan. "Have to be guns to fight great-grandfather. Right?"

"Exactly." Bolan smiled back. He thought he might just have an inkling as to what she was talking about. "Show me."

The Triple Witch

"EDGAR'S IN."

Craig sat back in his chair and contemplated the blue water as his ship knifed through it. "And what was our friend Edgar like?"

"I didn't have to kick his teeth in and he lives up to his billing. His men are absolute scum. You should have seen them. Swords, daggers, bandannas, puffy white shirts, the whole bit. There was even a guy with an eyepatch. The only thing missing was a peg leg and a parrot. You bought yourself one hundred genuine pirates of the Sulu Sea."

Craig was vaguely amused. "What's the status on Rutgers?"

"He and his men are in California. They'll be flying to

Honolulu and then on to the Solomon Islands. Their weapons are already being flown in from Singapore and will be waiting at the airport on their arrival. We've chartered them a boat, and they will proceed directly to Pa'ahnui." The woman's voice paused on the phone. "I'm concerned."

"About?"

"C of E. Ilya's cleaned up his act some, but I don't think he's ready for an attack."

Craig stared at the map of Pa'ahnui on his computer. "You think an attack is coming?"

"It's what I would do."

Craig considered that. The woman was his most trusted tactical adviser. "How many men does Ilya have?"

"He's taken some casualties. I'd say he has around one hundred effectives. On top of that, maybe two dozen Menzies security agents, though they're really more leg breakers than soldiers."

"What about weapons? Has Ilya set up an armory?"

"Yes, he's missing something like a dozen rifles and handguns. All spare weapons and munitions are being stored in the church cellar. The natives will have to breech all of our defenses and get to the middle of town to get at them. If they do that, then they're a moot point anyway."

"I agree. What about explosives?"

The natives managed to get some dynamite and blasting caps before we shut down the mining sites, but they didn't get much. For patrols we send out, booby traps could be a problem. In an attack mode, they'd be down to throwing lit sticks of dynamite. To do that, they have to get past the kill zone, the trench and the wire. So any explosives they have aren't likely to be problematic."

"So why are you worried?"

"Worrying is part of my job description," the woman replied.

"The Russian position is solid. Rutgers and Edgar are en route. The enemy has nothing to attack with but pointed sticks. What exactly has you worried?"

"That blue-eyed bastard who showed up on the island."

"What about him?"

"I don't like him. I don't like anything about him."

Craig smiled. "What is the situation with the reporter on the island?"

He could sense the woman smiling on the other end of the line. "She's gonna be a real pain in the ass."

"BAD PLACE, GI."

Bolan stood with a pick in his hand. He glanced at the two weathered human skulls mounted on posts. They were clearly a warning. "What's in there?" he asked.

"Ghosts." Sh'sho stared past the skulls, his face unreadable. "Nothing but hungry ghosts."

James, Si-Se and Hitihiti stepped back prudently. Red put his fists on his hips and glowered at the highlander. "Bullshit."

Sh'sho shrugged.

Beyond the warning totems, the Bad Place looked out westward across the Solomon Sea. It also looked down with palpable menace upon the Church of England.

Bolan had been on many battlefields. He had fought on strips of the earth that had known nothing but bloodshed for a thousand years. There were places that had history, that had resonance. Some were places of great power or holiness, drawing spiritualists to them like magnets. Others vibrated with fear and despair. Where Bolan stood, the wind moaned through blades of volcanic rock, and the mist crawled down the steep mountainside, slowly closing in. The trees were stunted and wind-twisted, like sculptured studies in anguish. High above, the volcano rumbled and oozed ash and smoke into the air.

Sh'sho was right.

It was a bad place.

Tactically, however, it was a perfect command post for warfare.

The place was an overgrown hillock, incongruously lumped against the side of the mountain. Bolan peered at it long and hard. He noted its shape underneath the decades of erosion from above, and his eyes pierced through half a century of jungle reclamation. Bolan made out obscured but identifiable man-made features.

The Bad Place was a bunker.

Once the firing slits were recognized, the thin, black, overgrown apertures stared back like empty eye sockets. Sh'sho stared into them steadily, then let out a long breath. "You go in, you lose your soul."

Sh'sho put his hand on Bolan's shoulder and pointed his club at the Imperial Japanese bunker. "Nothing but ugly, starving, spirits in there, boss. Sometimes, holy men come, put flowers or palm wine by door to appease them." He shook his head slowly. "My people no go in."

"I understand." Bolan nodded. "I'm going in."

Sh'sho sighed.

Bolan walked past the skull totems and approached the bunker. He knelt beneath a firing slit poked in the dirt. He found the corroded green tubes of rifle shells that had been ejected from the slits.

The place had been defended until the end.

"Red, bring the sledge."

"Right." Burdick stepped forward with a wooden maul of native manufacture in his fists. It took little time to locate the

door. They scraped away the dirt and dead vegetation. The big
man spit on his hands. "Step aside."

"It might be booby-trapped," Bolan said.

Burdick paused, looking at the bunker with renewed respect. "Fuck it. We don't have time to dig in from the roof."

The rotten beams of the ironbound door shattered under a
stroke of Burdick's sledge.

"Jesus!" Red flailed and swatted and Si-Se screamed as
bats burst shrieking out of the firing slits and the stoved-in
door. Bolan waited for the flapping black cloud to disperse
downslope into the jungle and then used the pick to clear the
rest of the door. He stepped back and stared into the beckoning blackness before him. "Si-Se."

The woman stepped leerily between the two skulls and
brought Bolan a torch. He struck a match to it and descended
into the dark.

The door had been massively thick, and a pair of equally
huge beams had been used to brace it against the native assault. Half a century of tropical humidity and insects had reduced the beams to rotting shells.

The stench of ammonia from fifty years of undisturbed bat
guano was overpowering. Bolan was half afraid the atmo-
sphere might ignite. It was a typical WWII strong point of the
Pacific Theater. The Japanese had neither the time nor the
tools to get concrete up this high on the mountain. The bunker
was constructed of heavy beams and rammed earth and but-
tressed with sandbags. It was furnished with a few tables and
chairs, and bunks along the back wall.

Bolan confronted the ghosts.

The dead lay contorted, calcified and frozen in time. Animals and insects had eaten them down to skeletons. The bats
hanging overhead had rained down upon them for years, coat-
ing them into distorted figures from a wax museum that had

been exposed to too much heat. The bodies were all headless. The rusted remnants of more than a dozen dirks lay close at hand to each corpse. The Japanese had committed *seppuku*, ritual suicide, rather than fall into the hands of their savage enemy. They had ripped their bellies with their daggers, proving they did not fear death, and then a *Kaishakunin*, or second, had given them final mercy with a beheading stroke of a sword. Skulls lay all around the room where they had rolled. Every pair of empty eye sockets seemed to watch Bolan as he entered the place of death.

One ghost still sat in place, sword in hand, waiting for the end of the world.

The corpse knelt against the far wall facing the door. He had been the last man. His corroded dagger lay at his knees, and he faced the door, waiting for the enemy, and he had done so since 1945.

Red stared over Bolan's shoulder. "Jesus."

"Yeah." The dead soldier before them represented a kind of personal duty and fortitude unknown in the new millennium.

"They must have gotten cut off, locked themselves in, and when no one came to relieve them…" Burdick shuddered.

Bolan nodded. He saw it the same way. "Si-Se is right. There should be weapons here. The Japanese would have been preparing to fight the Marines as they came up from the beach. Once your fellow jarheads had landed, they would have fought them through the jungle and every step up the mountain, trying to inflict as many casualties as possible. It was their standard tactic as the war turned against them in the Pacific.

"Right." Red grimaced. "But the enemy came out of the jungle behind them instead."

Bolan glanced around and found a skull leering at him

from the middle of the floor. The skull appeared to be sitting on a trapdoor. The skull came away from the floor with a snap as the brittle combination of dirt and excrement that held it broke. Bolan gave the skull a quick bow of his head and set it on a table.

Bolan and Red grabbed the iron ring on the floor and pulled. Half of the trapdoor came up with the ring and the other half collapsed inward.

Bolan went down another set of narrow steps. Throughout the Pacific, the Japanese had been inveterate tunnelers. The air was close and dry. No tropical air had penetrated, and no animals had invaded it. Bolan raised his torch and was greeted by the glint of metal.

Rifles were racked along the walls, and there were numerous stacked crates.

Red grinned as he stuck his head in the armory. "Jackpot."

"Hold this." Bolan handed Red his torch and took a rifle from one of the racks. The bolt action weapon was nine and a half pounds of wood and steel and more than four feet long. Bolan blew dust off the bolt and found rust and pitting along the barrel and dust cover. Red held the torch closer. Bolan squinted to read the markings. The rifle was a 38th year model standing for the 38th year of the Emperor Hirohito's reign. That had been in 1905 by the Western calendar. The rifles were made until the early 1940s.

Bolan opened the bolt. The action was gritty and sluggish with disuse but did not appear to be damaged. He shouldered the rifle and rammed the bolt home. The hammer dropped with a sharp click as he pulled the trigger. Bolan drew a bayonet from its sheath and fixed twenty inches of steel onto the rifle's muzzle. It had been a joke during the war in the Pacific that a Japanese soldier's weapon was taller than he was. It generally took only one Japanese suicide attack to stop the laughter. The Imperial Japanese Arisaka rifle would probably still do the job.

It would have to.

Red nodded at the antique weapon. "We're going on the warpath, aren't we?"

"Yeah." Bolan dismounted the bayonet and put the rifle back in the rack. "I want an inventory of everything in here within the hour. Then I want everything that's serviceable cleaned up and ready by morning."

"Really." Red had been transferred to Ordnance after an Iraqi mine had bounced him out of Force Recon. He obviously had reservations about the ancient iron surrounding him. "That's gonna take about a barrel of Hoppe's No. 5 solvent and a hundred liters of LSA gun lube."

"You can requisition two gallons of gasoline from the jeep Calvin stole and all the coconut oil the highlanders are willing to squeeze for you."

"Right. Gasoline, tanning butter and war relics." The big Marine smiled ruefully. "This is gonna be good."

9

The Highlands

"What have you got for me, Red?"

Burdick stood among a sea of dusty crates and weapons in various states of disrepair. Everywhere natives were scrubbing, filing and examining ordnance.

The big Marine took a stub of pencil from behind his ear and consulted the notepad the inspector had given him. "Okay, here's the situation. There were 150 rifles down there. I'd rate around a hundred of them to be in fair to good condition. The rest have pitted bores, weak springs, cracked stocks… They'll probably go bang the first few times you pull the trigger, but where the bullets go and how long they'll keep it up is highly questionable."

"What's the good news?"

"The good news is that all the rifle ammo was packed like canned hams. Took a church key to open them. So it should all still be in decent condition. We have one hundred 50 mm mortar bombs," but no way to deliver them."

Bolan examined the pile of bombs that were the bastard child of a hand grenade and a mortar projectile. "Yeah…but I see possibilities."

"Yeah, they got me thinking too. We have a few boxes of

some very unsafe-looking hand grenades and four heavy machine guns, only one of which I have any faith in."

"And?"

"Four submachine guns. All the pistol ammo is highly suspect. Got about a dozen Nambu pistols that I'd be leery about betting my life on. Two sniper rifles, one with decent optics."

"Give it to me," Bolan said.

"It's yours." Red glanced over at the villagers as they put edges on steel. "I've got about fourteen swords that cleaned up okay."

"Give one to anybody who doesn't have a rifle and bayonet," Bolan said.

"Right."

"What about machine guns?"

"We have two heavy and six light." Red spat on the ground. "Only one of each that I'd trust."

Bolan examined a string of iron shapes that resembled turn of the twentieth century train parts. "What are those?"

Red threw up his hands. "I'm not exactly sure. My guess is those are 70 mm pack howitzers."

Bolan stared at the pile of iron. "Really?"

"Yeah, as meaningful ordnance they're sad by modern standards, but that was the beauty of the Japanese system in WWII. A 50 mm mortar is barely more than a hand grenade. A 70 mm howitzer is a joke, but..." Red got excited as he warmed up to his subject. "All of this stuff broke down so that every man in the platoon carried a piece on top of his personal load. When the Japanese showed up for a fight on some jungle mountaintop they had these mortars and artillery pieces and the Dutch, the Brits and the U.S. did not."

Bolan stared at another mass of metal that still lay in its

crate. Whatever it was, it appeared to be nearly eight feet long. "What's that?"

Red waved his hands. "Man, I don't know. I thought it was an antitank rifle, but then I found a selector switch on it. Now I think it's an antitank machine gun. I don't know man."

"Tell me you can put this together," Bolan said.

Red gave the mass of parts a wary glance. "Dude, I speak Japanese. Reading 1942 instruction manuals in *kanji* is a whole lot different."

"I'll give you twenty-four hours."

Red's notepad went limp in his hand. 'Striker."

"Twelve."

"All right, fine, whatever. I'm on it."

"You know?" Bolan surveyed the sea of ancient ordnance. "Forget it."

"Forget it?"

"For the moment." Bolan looked around the village and weighed the options. Defensively they were few. They would have to rely on offense. "Tell Sho I want one hundred highlanders. The best he can find. Preferably young, in good shape and angry. I want the pick of the litter, and then you double-check them for fitness. I want them assembled here at dawn. Issue each man a rifle and a bayonet. Set their sights at one hundred yards. Give them the rudiments of marksmanship and one hundred rounds of practice ammo. When that's expended, put them through bayonet drills. Do that until noon and repeat the process after lunch."

"What about heavy machine gun teams or artillery squads?"

"We don't have time to train them."

"You want a raiding force."

Bolan looked at the sun. "In about forty-eight hours."

"Jesus! You think that's enough time?"

"We're out of time. It's coming down, Red, hard and soon."

Red had absolute faith in Bolan. "All right, I'm on it."

"Strikerman!" A native came loping out of the trees. "Hit-ihiti say trouble!"

"What kind of trouble?"

"Hitihiti say come see!"

"Red, you're in charge!" Bolan broke into a run and followed the highlander back into the jungle. It took fifteen minutes to run the overgrown path.

The Bad Place didn't look as bad as it used to. The skull totems had been removed. All of the firing slits had been cleared of undergrowth and debris. The interior of the bunker had been cleaned up. At James's suggestion the bodies had been removed, cremated, and the ashes wrapped in a faded Japanese flag retrieved from the bunker and buried in a cleared space. Highlanders had placed offerings of fruit and flowers over the grave. The hungry ghosts had been appeased, and ancient enemies honored.

From the air the bunker would still look like a lump, but it was now a fully functioning strong point. Truman Hitihiti stood by the edge of the precipice. He held a pair of Japanese naval artillery binoculars. He was looking down at the coast.

He was scanning Church of England.

"What have you got, Truman?" Bolan asked.

"Trouble, boss." He handed the binoculars to Bolan.

The Executioner scanned the town and his eyes were immediately drawn to the docks.

A small freighter had weighed anchor. Men were streaming off the ship like lines of ants. There were dozens of men. Scores of men. They were carrying rifles.

Bolan nodded. "We've got trouble."

Church of England

"WHO THE FUCK are you?"

Ilya Gaz stood surrounded by about seventy-five of his men and a dozen more Menzies agents. His men were dressed in khaki shirts, shorts and boots. To Gaz's eyes the town appeared to have been invaded by gypsies.

Heavily armed gypsies.

The men carried assault rifles and pistols and bladed weapons that curved in every direction.

The invaders slightly outnumbered Gaz, but he had the heavy weapons in his three remaining gun jeeps backing him up. They formed a hostile arc around the dock.

Edgar Gabriello glared at the Russian. "Who the fuck are you?"

"I am Ilya Gaz! *Commandant* Gaz, to you!"

Gabriello's smile was breathtakingly unpleasant. His eyes flicked around the fortified little town with meaning. "Where is Rutgers?"

"Fuck Rutgers! I am in command here!"

Gabriello's hand blurred. His palm cracked across Gaz's face with a sound like a cast-iron frying pan hitting a side of beef. The Russian reeled from the concussive force of the blow. His hand clawed for the 9 mm machine pistol thrust through the front of his belt.

"You fu—"

Two feet of undulating steel flashed. Gaz found the point of Gabriello's dagger pressed into the hollow of this throat. Gabriello smile was painted on his face as he pressed in and up, forcing Gaz to totter on his tiptoes. "You say something?"

The pirates laughed harshly at the Russian's predicament.

"No, tell me, white boy." Gabriello pressed harder with his blade. "What did you say?"

Blood leaked down between Gaz's collarbones. The Russian smiled and raised his voice so everyone could hear. "I said, Tomar, kill every one of these fucking monkeys on my dock."

The soldiers manning the gun jeeps racked the bolts on their general-purpose machine guns and 40 mm automatic grenade launchers. The selector lever of every Russian automatic carbine flicked to full-auto. The Filipino pirates leveled their rifles. The two forces faced each other in an apocalyptic Mexican standoff.

Edgar Gabriello threw back his head and laughed.

The sound was like a dog trying to bark and gargle blood at the same time. There was no humor in it. Nevertheless, the Russian soldiers and Filipino pirates relaxed slightly. They laughed nervously and fingers loosened on triggers all around. Gabriello slammed his dagger back into its sheath and took a step back. "I like you white boy, you're okay."

"Oh, I like you, too." Gaz rubbed the blood staining his chest.

"At ease!" Gaz ordered. He opened his arms and gave Gabriello a bloody kiss on each cheek. "Welcome to Pa'ahnui."

Gaz smiled. "Help yourself to whatever you need."

"I will." Gabriello pushed past and his men began to file off the docks.

Gaz turned to Marik. "You see that asshole?"

"Yeah?"

"I'm gonna cut off his arms and legs with an entrenching tool."

Marik nodded. He'd fought with Gaz in Chechnya. He'd seen him do it.

"But for now, I want a sniper on his ass at all times. Have Boris and Constantine take turns."

"Right."

Gaz wiped the blood from his mouth and his eyes fell upon his battered chair. "If that orangutan sits in my chair, shoot him."

10

"Long Point!"

Gleaming bayonets that had been honed to razor sharpness flashed. Straw spewed from the faces of the makeshift mannequins. Red marched up and down the line.

Bolan nodded. The ex-Marine was relishing the opportunity to be a drill instructor. That which had been visited upon him so long ago on Paris Island was now falling in spades upon the highlanders of Pa'ahnui.

They were thriving on it.

The highlanders were taking to bayonet fighting like ducks to water. They had grown up with spears in their hands and understood thrusting and parrying quite well. The buttstroke was new to them, but once Red demonstrated it all of them agreed it was genius.

Marksmanship was more problematic.

The majority of the highlanders could now hit a man-sized target at one hundred yards, but that was the extent of their skill. There was no time to turn them into combat riflemen. They were significantly better off than they had been with spears, but the equation was the same. To do damage, they were going to have to get in close.

"Sh'sho! Keep them at it for another half hour!" Red mopped his sweating brow and walked over to Bolan.

Bolan handed the sweating giant a coconut shell full of water. "They seem enthusiastic."

"Yeah." Red eagerly slurped the refreshment. Burdick gazed upon his little jarheads-in-gestation. "Enthusiasm they have in spades. Fire discipline, that's a whole 'other pot of poi. What you got is approximately two platoons of hemp smoking, pig farmers in skirts."

A pair of highlanders came running onto the practice field waving their arms and shouting at Bolan.

They turned to Red. Burdick, who was a master of many languages, had already developed a startling command of the local tongue. "They have news. Something about a reporter…I think."

Sh'sho trotted over and took a quick meeting with the two men. He still carried his pistol and his war club but now he also had a samurai sword tied across his back.

"Word comes from the valleys. Reporter on island. American. Russians very angry. Looking everywhere. Offering ten thousand for information where she is. Twenty for her alive. No want her to reach highlands."

"Has anyone seen this reporter?" Bolan asked.

The men waved their arms and pointed at Red. Sh'sho raised his hands helplessly. "Rumor say yes. Rumor say no. Rumor she have red hair. American. Name Juliet Thomas. Uhh…how you say? Reuters New Service."

"Reuters." Red scratched his chin thoughtfully. "She should at least have a cell phone."

Calvin James appeared in their little circle, grinning. "Stinks like a trap."

Bolan nodded. "Ask them where the rumors say this reporter's been seen."

Sh'sho listened a moment to the men and then pointed his war club down the mountain. "Rumor say pontoon plane landed on coast day ago. She been dropping money, asking to be taken to highlands. Rumor say she near north village this morning."

"Sho, Calvin." Bolan picked up one of the functioning submachine guns and a bayonet. "You're with me."

Church of England

"GET THE BITCH."

It was only the third time during his tenure on Pa'ahnui that Gaz had heard the voice of his employer. The voice on the other end of the line scared the shit out of him. "Rutgers hasn't arrived yet, shouldn't we get—"

"Get. The. Bitch." His employer spoke as if he were addressing a small child. "Which part of that did you fail to understand?"

"But…" Gaz stared out past the barbed wire and the trench. He really didn't want to leave the safety of the fortified township. He had no desire to go up into the highlands. Nothing good happened up there in the mist. He didn't want to leave Gabriello in command. "How the hell could a reporter get onto the island?"

"Ilya?"

"Uh…yes, boss?"

"Tell me, how can a bunch of primitive tribesmen with pointed sticks force over a hundred Russian veterans of Chechnya to hide behind their entrenchment?"

Gaz cleared his throat but beyond that he had no answer.

"Ilya?"

"Yes…boss."

"The American, he got past the Papuan naval blockade, didn't he?"

"Uh…yes."

"Truman Hitihiti and his two commando friends got past the Papuan naval blockade, didn't they?"

Gaz considered his answer. "Yes."

"You don't want to go out into the jungle do you." Craig was stating a fact.

Gaz paused.

"Tell you what you can do."

Gaz shuddered at the possibilities of what Craig might suggest he do with himself.

"Ilya?"

"Yes?"

"Send Edgar."

Gaz grinned.

He had no idea how much trouble he was in.

"GOTTA COME this way." Sh'sho shrugged. "If she want to make highlands."

The Ka'Kaio brothers nodded in agreement.

James looked out into the brush. "That assumes she has any idea she knows what she's doing."

"Let's assume she does," Bolan said. "Let's give her credit for bribing her way past the blockade, and assume she managed to ingratiate herself with some locals.

"Gotta come this way," the highlander reiterated. "Unless she totally lost, or dead. Or this ambush."

Sh'sho was right. There were very few obvious paths through the jungle. The one they were on had been traveled up and down the central mountain for thousands of years and was clear enough for any boy scout to follow. Once one was out of the valley the combination of jungle and surrounding steep terrain became almost impenetrable. Even someone totally lost would naturally follow the path.

Bolan lifted his head. "Someone's coming. Take cover."

James and the highlanders disappeared into the undergrowth. Bolan leaped and grabbed a branch above him. He swung himself up and swiftly clambered into the higher boughs. Iridescent butterflies the size of a man's hand fluttered from treetop to treetop in the tropical sunshine. It was a good vantage point on the path that formed a twisting, broken line up the mountain.

Bolan spotted a woman running for all she was worth.

Her red hair flew behind her and a knapsack bounced against her with every pound of her ground-eating stride. Her jaw was set in grim determination as she flew up the steep path. Bolan gazed out beyond her. He could see armed men trotting up the mountain trail behind her. They were not wearing the khaki shorts and shirts of the Russians. These men were wearing brightly colored Asian clothing and carrying assault rifles. Bolan flicked the safety off on his weapon.

These were the new guys.

Bolan spoke quietly to the shrubbery below. "A woman is coming. She's got some bad guys behind her. About a squad. I'm going to let her pass by. "Sh'sho, you and the brothers collect her." Bolan swung out of the tree. "Calvin, you're with me."

The two warriors loped a few yards down the mountainside and took cover behind shards of rock beside the path. It took only a moment before footfalls could be clearly discerned thudding on trail.

The woman flew past.

Bolan let her get a few yards farther then spoke. "Juliet."

The woman spun and nearly tripped on the loose rocks. She skidded and righted herself. She held a canister of pepper spray and thrust it out. Her blue eyes flared and her jaw dropped in surprise as she took in the two heavily armed men she had just run past.

Dark arms reached out of the trees and yanked the woman into the shrubbery.

"They're coming." James was peering between the blades of rock.

Bolan reached into his pocket and pulled out a crusted, sweating, rusted sixty-year-old hand grenade. "You want one?"

James shook his head as he examined the grenade Bolan tossed to him. The brass fuse casing on top had turned a waxy green. The pin was a piece of wire attached to a loop of ratty cording. Bolan pulled out a matching piece of beleaguered ordnance.

James glanced through a crack in his cover and held up five fingers. He began closing his hand one finger at a time.

Bolan could hear men trotting and cursing.

James made a fist.

Bolan yanked the cord, and it snapped in two in his hand. James gestured frantically. Bolan bit into the corroded wire and ripped the safety pin out with his teeth. He lobbed the grenade high over his cover and took up his submachine gun.

The grenade clanked to the ground and men shouted in alarm. Bolan recognized words in Tagalog.

James rolled his eyes as the grenade failed to go off. He whipped the muzzle of his weapon around the rocks and fired a burst down the path. Automatic rifles hammered in response.

Bolan dropped prone and rolled into the middle of the path.

Eight men had thrown themselves down and had risen to crouches when the grenade failed. Bolan sighted on the discolored lump of iron and fired. Dust and pebbles flew with bullet strikes and then sparks shrieked off the grenade. Bolan rolled behind cover as the grenade detonated with a crack and men screamed.

James leaned out from behind cover and his submachine gun rattled off a burst. One of the pirates staggered as his chest was cratered. The ancient Japanese 8 mm ammo had been anemic on the day of manufacture, but James put five rounds into the man in a pattern the size of a coffee cup. James swung his aim onto his next target, but nothing happened as he squeezed the trigger. He racked the bolt and raised the weapon to his shoulder. One round went off and the gun locked up tight.

"Shit!" James cast the weapon away and dived back as rifle bullets ripped into the rocks by his head. He drew his Heckler & Koch .45-caliber P-9 pistol.

Bolan fired a burst around the rocks, then his weapon jammed. "Grenade!"

James pulled the pin and tossed the ancient explosive.

The pirates shouted in alarm as the grenade bounced among them. Bolan drew a pistol from his belt and narrowed his eyes as the grenade failed to detonate. He whipped his head and arm around cover and fired at the lead attacker. Bolan's bullet smashed into the rifle and struck sparks off the action. His second bullet hit the pirate in the chest. Bolan's third round stovepiped in the action and his gun jammed.

"Damn." Bolan leaned away from the answering gunfire. He picked up his deactivated submachine gun and clicked the bayonet in place.

The remaining pirates let out a roar and charged.

The remaining grenade suddenly detonated and the battle roars instantly changed to screams. James came out of cover with his .45 hammering in his right hand. The wasp-waisted blade of a Gerber Mk II fighting knife glittered in his left. Pirates fell as the deep, hollowpoint .45-caliber rounds hit them like flying ashtrays.

Bolan lunged with his bayonet.

The pirate had his own bayonet fixed and they crossed blades. Bolan's opponent had the longer weapon and the Executioner returned into the attack. He went body to body to jam the pirate's weapon and thrust his own blade down through the man's sandaled foot. The pirate's scream was cut off as Bolan ripped the steel butt plate of his weapon into the pirate's jaw and shattered it.

He shoved the killer away and sliced the edge of the bayonet blade across the man's throat. James had his blade buried in a pirate's chest. He twisted it free and let the man fall. His .45 was empty.

The pirates were all down. Bolan glanced down at one who was moaning. The Japanese grenades were concussion weapons with little fragmentation. The Filipino's nose was bleeding and his eyes were rolling in his head. Bolan took a length of cord from his pocket and hog-tied the stunned pirate.

"Sho! Come on down, pick up the rifles and ammo. Bolan glanced up from his charge. "Sho!"

Bolan picked up a fallen rifle. "Cover me."

James picked up a weapon as Bolan went up the path. Bolan stepped into the underbrush and stopped. Sho was on his knees clutching a broken nose. The Ka'Kaio brothers were on their feet, but they were clutching their faces gagging and coughing with tears streaming down their faces.

The woman had her back against a tree. Her canister of pepper spray was dripping in her hand. She frantically jerked her chemical deterrent to point at one highlander and then another. A few feet away her rucksack lay open with the contents spilled out.

"You're Juliet Thomas?" Bolan asked.

The woman jumped and pointed the can at Bolan. He slowly raised his rifle overhead. "I surrender."

The woman shook with adrenaline reaction. "Um... you're..."

"We're the revolution."

11

The woman thrust her chin defiantly.

Sh'sho and the Ka'Kaio brothers had rifled through the contents of her rucksack with more vigor than necessary. A laptop fell to the grass followed by a tape recorder, batteries, a compact video camera and tapes. The woman made an unhappy noise as they poked and pawed through the interior pocket holding her personal items. Sh'sho sifted through the pile and shrugged. "She got no guns."

The woman stared at Bolan.

He was looking at her Reuters News Service ID, her passport and her California driver's license. They seemed to be in order, and the passport was well weathered and stamped with seals of nations throughout the Pacific Rim. They had taken her into the highlands, but they had gone to the Ka'Kaio brothers' village instead of Sh'sho's. A number of men here were carrying rifles from the Japanese cache, but no one was engaging in mass bayonet drills or trying to piece together WWII pack howitzers.

"Your beat is the South Pacific?"

"It used to be Europe. But I married a French guy and we moved to Tahiti." She shrugged. "It didn't work out. He left. I liked the islands. My daughter liked them. I stayed."

Bolan examined a picture of a grinning, unshaved man and

Thomas on the beach. They held a redheaded girl of no more than two or three in their arms.

Thomas read Bolan's mind. "She's four now. She's with my mother in Hawaii. A single woman has to work." She spoke through clenched teeth as the Ka'Kaio brothers stretched the elastic of a red silk thong and smiled delightedly as the garment sprang away from their fingers and landed on a shrub. "Can I have my underwear back?"

Bolan waved away the highlanders and Thomas began angrily shoving her things back into her pack.

"You're here to cover the revolution?" Bolan asked.

"I was here to cover the situation. Everyone outside thinks there's a Communist insurgency here. Then the Russians started raping and killing everything that moved. A villager down in the valley told me there was a price on my head, with the caveat they could do anything they wanted to me as long as they brought me in alive. At that point I decided to get some altitude."

James smiled. "I like her."

Thomas ran her eye in appreciation over the ex-Navy SEAL's scarred and chiseled torso. "I like you."

James waggled his eyebrows at the Executioner.

Bolan continued. "What can you tell me about the opposition?"

"The Russians? They're acting like they're on busman's holiday in Bosnia. I don't know who those other yahoos chasing me were but—"

"I mean Stephen Craig."

"That is one serious son of a bitch you're messing with. He made his first billion in the United States and found U.S. business law too confining. He went international, looking for opportunities that other businessmen would shudder to contemplate. He's a Second World economy onto himself. His bank account is bigger than the gross national product of a lot of the countries he messes with, and he makes people disappear. You're…" She looked back at James. "And just who are you, if you don't mind my asking? CIA? Naval Intelligence?"

"I'm with the Black Panthers." James held up his fist. "Oceania Chapter."

Sh'sho and the Ka'Kaio brothers held up their fists solemnly.

Juliet Thomas looked at Bolan. "And you?"

Bolan gave the power salute.

The reporter blew a lank red curl from her brow. "This just keeps getting better and better."

Bolan glanced at the battered notebook computer as she shoved it back in with her belongings. "You got a wireless Ethernet connection with that?"

"Oh yeah." She reached into a side pocket and pulled out a wireless base connection. The plastic box had a neat .22-caliber bullet hole punched through it.

Bolan sighed. "Cell phone?"

"Battery's dead."

"What do you know about the Russians?"

"They're being lead by a man named Gaz. Ilya Gaz. Former Russian airborne. Now he's a merc. He's—"

"I've heard of him." Ilya Gaz was on file at the Farm. Stony Man kept tabs on all active mercenary outfits. The Russian wasn't on the front burner of any Farm operations, but his activities qualified him for Bolan's attention. His presence explained a lot about how things had gone down on the island. "Calvin, find Miss Thomas a hut, let her freshen up and get her something to eat and drink."

"Wait! But—" The reporter took a step forward, but James laid a restraining hand on her shoulder.

"Sho." Bolan turned and walked across the village with the highlander in tow. Villagers grinned and waved at him. Bolan moved toward a hut on the opposite side of the village. A bass voice boomed in barely restrained rage. The bamboo walls of the hut shuddered as something bounced off them.

Bolan pushed through the hanging fabric of the door.

Trevor Burdick was calling down wrath and thunder from the heavens in Tagalog. Big Red pressed the Filipino pirate over his head and hurled him. The bound pirate bounced against the buckling wall and rolled back to the mats on the floor. Red examined the crumpled pile of pirate at his feet. "I have had enough of this shit!"

The pirate was curled into a ball on the floor, clutching himself with his bound hands and gobbling in mindless terror. He'd gotten Red's message. Truman Hitihiti squatted beside him speaking Tagalog in a quiet fatherly tone, like a priest imploring a sinner to save himself.

"One minute!" Red roared.

The pirate shrieked and suddenly began vomiting forth words in a rush. Hitihiti squatted back down, patting the pirate on the shoulder consolingly as he wept and betrayed and shuddered like a squid.

Bolan stepped out of the hut.

Hitihiti came out a few minutes later. "Well, they got about a hundred men. Automatic rifles. Didn't show up with much in the way of light support. They're pirates, being led by Edgar Gabriello. Some woman came and hired them, flashing big money, to help out dealing with the insurrection here on the island. I know Gabriello. Did some business with him once, bad business. He's a real bad man."

It was bad enough, but pirates were used to raiding coastal villages and taking vessels unaware late in the night. Their discipline as soldiers fighting a jungle warfare campaign of any duration was highly suspect. A bloody nose could send them packing.

James came running through the village. He did not look happy.

"What's up, Cal?" Bolan asked.

"We got a runner from the coast-watching team up on the bluff. They say a boat arrived, small one, yacht size. Some white men got off."

"How many?"

"Seven or eight."

Bolan glanced back at the hut. "Truman, did your friend say anything about expecting anybody."

"Yeah, he said Gabriello, the Russians, they were holing up in town, waiting on some white man. Strange name. Rut, Rutter, Rutgah...something."

The wind up the highlands suddenly blew cold. "Rutger Rutgers?"

"Yeah, kinda. Rutger Rutger," Hitihiti confirmed. "The pirate kept saying the name twice."

"And about seven or eight white men got off the boat with him?"

"Yeah."

James read the look on Bolan's face. "This is bad, isn't it?"

"Yeah." Bolan nodded slowly. "This is bad."

RUTGERS STEPPED OFF the gangplank surrounded by his team. Each man carried a locked and loaded Beretta BM-59 assault rifle slung over his shoulder. Rutgers immediately took in the field fortifications around the town with approval. He had been assured the place would be cleaned up by the time he arrived. Someone had stepped in and done some ass kicking.

Two men stood on the wharf to meet him. One was a short, heavily muscled Filipino he did not recognize. The other man was of the same stature, but with the wiry physique of a hardened veteran. The Russian offered him a sloppy salute that Rutgers did not return.

Rutgers new Ilya Gaz by reputation.

His atrocities in Chechnya were well documented, as were his activities working with the Serbs in Bosnia and an equally brutal stint in the Congo. His specialties were kidnapping, torture, mayhem, and the ruthless suppression of the opponent's civilian population. However there were numerous regions in the world where a ruthless outsider with Gaz's proclivities was needed. Mercenary work was at best a moral gray area. Rutger Eugenius Rutgers represented the professional mercenary profession in its best light.

Ilya Gaz represented the absolute cancer-blackened ass end of it.

Gaz exposed his gums in an ugly smile.

Rutgers smiled back thinly. He was not here to put up with any bullshit. He had come to win. His future was at stake.

Bryce Delvoix snorted at Rutgers's side. His telepathy had already kicked in. A single look at the situation and he understood his unwritten orders on the subject of Ilya Gaz implicitly.

"What are you fucking looking at?" Gaz said, challenging Delvoix.

"Nothing." The Boer's pale blue eyes did not blink. "Nothing at all."

Rutgers considered the man beside Gaz. "You are Captain Gabriello, then?"

The pirate blinked. It wasn't an honorific he was used to. "Yes." He grinned apishly. "I'm captain."

"Good, tell me. Where are you holding the reporter?"

Gabriello looked away uncomfortably.

Rutgers sighed.

Gaz sneered. "*Captain* Gabriello let her get away. Lost twelve of his men in the attempt," he added. "The highlanders are probably barbecuing them as we speak."

Gabriello's hand was on his knife.

Rutgers ignored the spat. "How many men do we have in total?"

Gaz did math on his fingers. "About eighty-eight of Edgar's crew, about 120 or so of mine if none of the pricks have gotten themselves killed today. Maybe twenty Menzies men, that's—"

"Two hundred and thirty men, approximately," Rutgers said. It would be more than enough.

"I want all the men not on the perimeter assembled for inspection in forty-five minutes," Rutgers ordered.

Gabriello blinked. Gaz opened his mouth. "Listen here, Rut—"

The Dutchman's voice was hard. "Commander Rutgers, Senior-Lieutenant Gaz."

Gaz grimaced. He almost choked on the word. "Commander."

"Forty-five minutes." Rutgers gazed up into the mists of the highlands. "I want all forces ready to assault in forty-eight hours."

12

Bolan sipped banana beer and considered his battle plan. The night was pitch-black as another summer squall pounded Pa'ahnui. A single coconut oil lamp lit his hut. He lay in a low hammock and scanned Burdick's inventory list for the hundredth time. There were far too many question marks scratched next to the list of Japanese antiquities they had dug from the bunker.

Bolan considered his cannons.

Red had been cannibalizing parts and hoped to have at least one, possibly two functioning pack howitzers by dawn. Those could turn the tide of battle. They had one heavy and one light machine gun. Those weapons would be their only answer to the enemy's helicopter. They would have to suck the chopper in close with something irresistible, probably himself, and Bolan's barely trained machine gun crews would have only one chance to knock the chopper out of the sky before they got ripped to pieces by the answering fire.

In the end, the whole thing was going to hinge on surprise and one suicidal bayonet charge.

Bolan's hand closed around the grips of a Spanish Astra Falcon pistol. They'd netted twelve Chinese automatic rifles and an assortment of handguns from the battle with the pirates on the mountain trail. They needed more, but the enemy was holing up tight in town

In the morning he and James would see about coaxing a few of them out from their entrenchments.

Bolan pushed off the Astra's thumb safety as the veranda outside his hut creaked with human weight. The highlanders didn't have doors or windowpanes. They just hung fabric to keep out mosquitoes. Nevertheless, someone knocked lightly on the rattan door frame.

Bolan flicked the safety back on and tucked the pistol away. "Come on in, Juliet."

Juliet Thomas pushed aside the fabric. The tropical rain fell heavily and took only a few seconds to soak a person. The reporter's white T-shirt clung to her curves like a translucent second skin.

She shook her head in amused irritation. "How did you know it was me?"

"You're the only person who would knock. Calvin, Red and Truman would've called out so I wouldn't shoot them, and the highlanders don't give a damn. They just walk right in and expect something to eat."

She looked into his eyes with great seriousness. "You think you stand a chance?"

"Maybe."

She looked at the pistol resting on his lap and then at the antique sniper rifle in the corner and the sword sheathed next to it. "I took a walk around the village today."

"Oh?"

"I counted about seventy-five grown men."

"And?"

"And less than half had a rifle. Less than half of them had anything more modern than that museum piece over there. I've been through the coastal areas and one of the river valleys. The people are angry and ready to fight." She shook her head. "But you'd better have something up your sleeve."

"Guts?" Bolan offered. "Determination?"

"You think that's enough? Against Gaz? Against Gabriello?"

"Gabriello's men are pirates and Gaz's men are mercs of the lowest kind. You give them stiff resistance, you let them know that ten of you are willing to die just to scratch one of them, and they'll go into 'we didn't sign up for this shit mode.' The wild card is Rutgers. With him on the island these guys will develop backbone, whether they want to or not. Then again, Rutgers is a professional. He'll see a no-win situation quicker than the pirates and thugs." Bolan paused. "It all comes down to Craig. He's a businessman. I don't think we have to win, we just have to turn the situation unprofitable. Craig sees that and he'll cut his losses and go find himself a new situation."

"From everything I've learned a real asshole this Craig guy is. The kind of asshole who doesn't take no for an answer."

Bolan shrugged with grim finality. 'Then he's a dead man."

The woman's eyes went wide. "You think so?"

"I've seen firsthand what he's unleashed on this island." Bolan nodded slowly.

The rain rattled on the roof in the sudden silence. Thunder boomed not far overhead.

Thomas shivered.

"Sorry." Bolan's eyes warmed. "Didn't mean to scare you."

"You didn't scare me," she said, blushing. "Actually, that tough guy stuff turns me on." She sat beside him in the hammock.

Bolan took in Juliet's body. A blue-eyed redhead with a deep tan was a rarity. Her long hair spilled across his arm. Her skin pressed against his bare shoulder and side. Her perfectly turned calf rubbed against his with each swing of the hammock. The wet T-shirt clung to her curves. He was tempted, but he didn't respond.

"Oh my God, a genuine gentleman." Her lashes fluttered

provocatively. "You're thinking it would be wrong to take advantage of me."

"A little," Bolan conceded. "You've been through a lot lately." He took in her smile. "What are you thinking?"

"I'm thinking I'm a single mom who's never made love in a hammock."

Bolan blew out the lamp and coconut scented smoke drifted in the darkness. A sodden T-shirt squished as it hit the floor. Flesh filled both of Bolan's hands as the knot of his sarong was unraveled. The hammock swung like a pendulum and she seized his shoulders so she wouldn't topple out. "Damn it! How do we do this?"

"You know the natives don't do it in hammocks. They just sleep in them. If they want good lovin', they go off in the bushes like decent people."

"I'm perverted." Her hands moved across his body. "And I'm on a mission."

Bolan reached down and laid his pistol on the floor. "Okay, but this is going to get complicated, and possibly dangerous."

Her lips brushed Bolan's ear in a throaty whisper. "I can take direction."

BOLAN ROSE BEFORE DAWN. The reporter had crept from the hammock late in the night after the rain had stopped. She had said nothing so Bolan had feigned sleep and let her go. The hammock had been quite an experience. Juliet Thomas had done much more than take direction. She had proved downright resourceful.

Bolan stepped out onto the veranda. Calvin James sat on a log watching the volcano turn black as the orange light of the rising sun limned it from behind. He glanced up at Bolan from a cup of the steaming weeds the natives passed for tea. He pointed an accusing finger. "Man…she was mine."

Bolan yawned and stretched. "She came to my hut, Cal."

James shrugged and rose. "What's on the agenda for the day?"

"We need more guns, and I want to probe the enemy defenses. Piss them off, give them an opportunity to make some mistakes. Maybe draw out their helicopter and shoot the shit out of it."

James eyed the rifle Bolan held in his hand. "Sniper mission?"

"You down with that?"

James nodded. "I'll go get the binoculars."

"I'll wake Red and let him in on the plan."

Except for a few guards with rifles, the village still slept. Bolan stopped by the reporter's hut. He was about to knock on the door frame when he heard the very soft, rapid sound of clicking keys. His hand went to the fabric hanging over the door and found it had been tied down. Bolan's bayonet came soundlessly out of his sarong. The razor-sharp steel parted the cord holding one side of the fabric.

Bolan stepped inside the hut.

Thomas sat cross-legged in front of her laptop. Her fingers were a blur on the keyboard. Bolan noted that the Ethernet connection with the bullet hole in it was plugged in, and a component he did not recognize was attached to it.

But the component had a short antenna. At the top of it was a miniature folding parabolic dish like an aluminum sunflower.

Bolan doubted the rig had the power to reach Reuters in London. For that matter it would not be able to reach the Solomon Islands or Port Moresby in Papua. A transmitter that small would need a local base station with an Internet connection to relay off a satellite.

The only possible local base station on Pa'ahnui would be in the Church of England, and it would be in Russian hands.

The video camera lay in two halves. The body of the camera had been an empty shell, and had been used to smuggle in the transmitter and God only knew what else, but Bolan suspected that his hut and probably half the village were wired for sound by now.

The woman's head flew up as Bolan entered. Her eyes flicked to the transmitter unit and then to Bolan and the blade he held. She made no attempt at pretense or denial. Her blue eyes simply glared at Bolan with startlingly glacial, insane hatred.

Bolan spoke very quietly. "I want you to recline backward very slowly, until you're lying on your back. Then roll onto your stomach, and keep your hands at your sides.

Her hand flicked to her components and closed around a metal case shaped like an oversized videocassette. Bolan reversed the knife in his hand as she grabbed the metal cassette in both hands and yanked it apart. One half clicked back to form a rudimentary buttstock. From beneath the other half the pistol grip and loaded magazine dropped down into position.

Bolan flung the bayonet as the Russian PP-90 deep-concealment submachine gun burned into life in Juliet's hand. The twenty-inch bayonet blade rotated through the air in a metal blur. Heat seared Bolan's thigh and biceps and his hand went numb around his pistol. The bayonet sank into the woman's shoulder. She grimaced and her aim went high as her arm spasmed. The miniature submachine gun snarled itself empty through the roof of the hut. She pulled the blade free.

Bolan ignored his fallen pistol and lunged.

She had already rolled backward and popped to her feet, and she ripped the transmitter component out of the laptop as she went. She scooped something off the floor and flung herself backward before Bolan could lay his hands on her. Fabric tore as she leaped through the window. Bolan dived after her and hit the morning mud rolling.

Thomas was on her feet and running.

Burdick came around the corner, his eyes wide at the scene.

"Red!" Bolan came to his feet. " Stop her!"

Burdick threw a massive left-handed haymaker at her jaw. The woman slipped the blow and Red's fist smashed through the wall of the hut. Her own ridge-hand blow swung between Red's legs like a blunt ax. He gagged and buckled.

The entire exchange took but a heartbeat.

She was still moving.

Bolan vaulted Burdick's agonized form as the woman accelerated away down a lane between a pair of pig enclosures.

Truman Hitihiti suddenly filled the lane to block her path. His hamlike hands shot out to grab her.

She jumped, legs scissoring.

The Tongan had just enough time to blink as her first and second kick literally walked up his chest. He staggered as her body torqued around. Her right heel clouted him across the jaw, and he sprawled across a low fence and dropped among the squealing swine.

Thomas Juliet landed running.

Dogs were barking and people were rushing out of their huts. The woman's head turned once to check Bolan's progress and she accelerated even more. Bolan grimly gave chase. The wound in his leg was already burning with each step.

The wound in her shoulder did not seem to be affecting her stride in the slightest.

They passed out of the village and ran through the trees.

"Striker!" James called from not far behind.

Bolan lengthened his stride and sprinted all out.

The woman's head turned. Bolan was gaining. The trail through the forest plateau suddenly plunged downward into a mountain path. Juliet Thomas raced down it like a gazelle.

The Executioner followed her.

A moment later the gray metal cylinder of a white phosphorus grenade clattered to the rocky path. Bolan threw himself off the path and crashed though the wall of solid jungle. The grenade popped and whooshed as it sent white-hot streamers of smoke and burning phosphorus like a Fourth of July display. The jungle reached out spitefully, clawing and lashing at Bolan as he rolled down the mountainside. He continued to roll, putting distance between himself and the burning death raining down. The jungle canopy above sizzled and popped as the burning metal met the wet foliage. If the white phosphorus landed on him, water would not put it out. The molten metal would cling to his flesh and continue to burn.

Bolan bounced to a jarring stop against a tree trunk.

Choking white smoke bloomed and mated with the mist on the mountain above. The black smoke of burning jungle undergrowth was swiftly mixing with it. Bolan heaved a ragged breath. He had managed to fall down the mountain out of the lethal range of the falling phosphorus.

"Striker!" James's voice boomed.

Bolan rose to a crouch and scanned his surroundings. Juliet Thomas—or whoever she was—was wounded, and most likely doing distance. But Bolan had seen the woman in action, and he did not put it past her to double back and try to finish him off.

"Striker!"

Bolan picked up a fist-sized rock and made his way back to the trail. Smoke and fire blocked the mountain path. Bolan peered down the misty slopes. He caught movement through a break in the morning fog. His first assessment had been correct. Thomas showed no sign of slowing.

"Striker!"

"Yeah!" Bolan took a ragged breath. "I'm all right!"

"Juliet?"

Blood leaked down Bolan's leg. "Gone."

"Can you make your way back up?"

"No!" Bolan shouted. "Meet me in the East River valley! Bring your medical kit. Bring my rifle and the equipment we'll need, and come quick!"

There was a trace of amusement in James's voice. "The morning mission goes on as planned?"

"If Red can still walk, tell him to get his team ready and in position!" Bolan watched the fleeing figure disappear into the mist far below. "We counterattack immediately."

Church of England

Lizabet Smakofani walked up to the Russian pickets before they knew she was there. They jumped as a unit when she spoke in Russian. "I am unarmed. I am—"

"The reporter!" one guard shouted. He lunged to grab her.

She thumbed the Russian in the throat and dropped him wheezing to his knees. She wheeled on his comrade. "You, tell me. Has Rutgers arrived?"

The man clutched his rifle uncertainly.

"You don't remember me?"

The Russian blinked as he saw past the blue contact lenses and the long red hair extensions. *"Da!"* He grinned delightedly as he suddenly understood. "You were spying!"

"That's right." She nodded tolerantly. "Now why don't you escort me into town so I don't have to kick the shit out of anyone else."

The guard fell into step, and they marched from the jungle picket toward the cleared no-man's land surrounding the town. The guard shouted out the call sign and they marched through the barbed wire and sharpened stakes of the kill zone.

"Fetch a medic." She broke off from the guard and walked

into the Menzies Mining office. The guards inside had seen her walk up from the window but were not sure what to do. They stared at her bloody shoulder as she walked up the stairs.

Rutgers stood behind a desk. Edgar Gabriello and two white men she did not recognize were with him. The Dutchman nodded slowly. "Our Trojan horse, he said."

The woman nodded. "When did you figure it out?"

"We detected you when you went active on the wireless link this morning." His eyes were slightly reproachful. "Of course, the information you sent was encrypted, and not intended for me, but what was happening was easy enough to deduce."

"You…" Gabriello did some math. "You got my men killed! On purpose!"

She tossed her head dismissively. "Attempts to kill or capture me were necessary for my cover."

Rutgers raised an eyebrow. "But what if Gaz or Gabriello's men had shot or killed you?"

"I considered that a distant possibility at best."

"Please, sit down. You are bleeding. May I get you something to drink?" Rutgers reached into a small refrigerator and brought out a bottle of South African sauvignon blanc and uncorked it. He poured a glass as the medic arrived. "Would you share your report?"

The woman didn't flinch as the Russian medic cleaned and probed the wound. She sipped her wine as he began stitching. "I saw only one village before I was compromised. I believe there are four or five up there, though much smaller than the valley and coastal settlements."

"What did you see there?"

"Three Special Forces operators are in command. The same three as mentioned in your situation report. I have confirmed that they are all Americans, but what branch of service or the U.S. government they represent, if any, is unclear. My first impression is that they are acting independently. Truman Hitihiti, the smuggler, is with them and cooperating. So I am assuming he has actively joined the revolutionary forces."

"What kind of armament did you observe?"

"On first contact the commandos had some malfunctioning submachine guns and some equally unreliable hand grenades. They looked like antiques. I noticed a number of very old bolt-action rifles among the natives as well. They must be WWII surplus. Everything else they have is captured from us, and that is limited to a few dozen automatic rifles and handguns. The rest are armed with spears."

Rutgers nodded. The news was good. Very good. "I assume you can find the village again?"

"Yes, the paths up the mountain are fairly clear if you know where to find them. The paths between the highland villages should be equally obvious."

"I am considering launching an assault within the hour."

The woman smiled with genuine warmth. "Really."

"Yes." Rutgers poured himself a glass of wine and took a seat on the couch. He gazed out the window toward the cloud-shrouded volcano that loomed over everything. "I wish to have at least one of the highland villages pacified and a mountain base camp established before nightfall. The reduction of the rest of the highlands should proceed rapidly after that."

"Very aggressive."

"I wish to end the guerrilla warfare phase of this campaign. It should never have been allowed to begin."

"I concur."

"Lizabet, your report confirms that the revolutionary forces in the highlands cannot stand up to a concentrated attack. I want the Russians broken into squads, each led by one of my men. I wish to finish this war, now, with one massive blow from which they cannot recover."

"The paths are steep and treacherous. They will attempt ambushes."

"We will dismount the automatic grenade launchers from the vehicles and bring them with us. The helicopter will direct fire."

"Do it," she said.

Rutgers sipped his wine. "Craig will authorize it?"

"I am authorizing it. Your appraisal is correct. The time for tit-for-tat raids is over. It is time for open warfare. We take the highlands." She finished her wine. "We take the initiative. We strike the first blow, and we strike the last one."

The window shattered into flying shards, and Tymon Corboline's head exploded like a ruptured melon. Blood misted the air of the office, and flying brain and flecks of bone painted the walls in a sweeping mural of abstract gore. The tracker's binoculars fell from nerveless fingers and his nearly decapitated corpse toppled across the command desk.

Rutgers seized the woman and pulled her to the floor with him as he hit the deck. "Sniper!"

Gabriello dropped down beside them. His right-hand man, Flores, watched in frozen horror as the headless South African oozed blood and bodily fluids across the desk. Flores staggered as some terrible unseen fist plowed into his chest. Blood flew from his mouth and nose as his heart burst under the bullet's impact. The sound of the distant rifle shot was clear through the shattered window.

Flores fell to the floor.

Automatic weapons began firing along the trenches.

The first blow had been struck. The initiative had been taken.

"It's the commando. He had a sniper rifle in his hut," the woman said.

Rutgers reacted. "Bryce, take Valdemar and Jensen. You're on the ground. "Put Piet and Kiins in the helicopter. I want this sniper before sundown."

Bryce Delvoix pushed himself up from the floor. "I'll bring you his head."

BOLAN CHAMBERED a fresh round and belly crawled to his next firing position. Calvin James crawled alongside him. Tracers streaked through the trees, and grenades were raining down blindly through the jungle canopy. The enemy had not detected exactly where he had fired from, but they sure as hell would have their eyes wide open now.

They sprawled in their next arranged position behind a clump of rocks that offered cover and a perfect firing lane through the trees to the enemy watchtower. Bolan arranged himself around the rifle. The stock was too short and the fixed 2.5 power scope set too far back, but the average height of Japanese soldiers in WWII had been well below Bolan's. The soldier craned his neck and sighted on the church steeple. He examined the man behind the sandbagged machine-gun emplacement and then put his crosshairs on the man with the Dragunov semiautomatic sniper rifle scanning the tree line. "Range me."

Calvin James scanned the target with the ancient Japanese Royal Navy artillery binoculars. "Range, 620 meters. Wind from the right…" James estimated the offshore breeze by the palm fronds behind the watchtower. "Ten miles per hour."

Bolan altered his aim just slightly. His finger slowly began to take up slack on the trigger. The rifleman's mantra moved unconsciously through his mind. Don't pull the trigger, squeeze it. The rifle's fire should come as a surprise to the shooter as well as the target. Squeezing…squeezing… squee— The rifle cracked and bucked against Bolan's shoulder.

"Hit!" James said.

The sniper in the tower jerked and sagged across his sandbags. His rifle slipped from his spasming hands and clattered to the ground below. The machine gunner screamed and began ripping bursts into the jungle blindly.

Bolan and James were already up and sprinting through the trees. They could hear the automatic grenade launchers and hugged dirt as high-explosive grenades began detonating in the treetops.

A heavier, rhythmic thumping shook the air.

James flipped the selector lever on his commandeered assault rifle to full-auto. "Chopper," he said, warning Bolan.

The Executioner kept his eyes on the single road leading out of the fortified town. "They're deploying a team. Countersniper."

Jeeps were rolling out. Heavily armed men hung from the roll bars like apes. They went off road and came in a fairly straight line toward Bolan and James's.

"Someone judged the angle of that last shot of yours pretty damn precisely," James said.

"We're up against Executive Options men now. The mucking around is over," Bolan replied.

The armed Dauphin helicopter clawed into the sky. James cocked his head as he gauged the rotor noise. "He's flying on one engine. Looks like you and Red did him some damage they haven't been able to repair."

Bolan noted the loaded rocket boxes beneath the lateral armament pylons. The damage hadn't been enough. Executive Options was sending out a full platoon in the antisniper role, and they had air support.

Bolan and James had one very dodgy surprise up their sleeves, and if it failed, they would be dead meat under the onslaught of the South African mercenaries.

"MOVE! MOVE! MOVE!"

Red, Truman, Sh'sho and the Ka'Kaio brothers jogged down the jungle path. A half-dozen highlanders carrying rifles and lattices woven with brush and vines followed. Truman and the highlanders grunted as they carried the Type 92 heavy machine gun between them. The Japanese army had installed sockets in the feet of all of their tripod served weapons, so that the crew could slide poles through and carry the weapons fully assembled and ready to fire. Red's gun crew slid spears through the sockets, and the weapon bounced and flexed on the edge of disaster as they manhandled the machine gun down the mountain. Red ran point, cradling his Type 96 light machine gun. All of them were festooned with spare magazines and clips of ammo. Red checked his watch and picked up the pace. Gunfire echoed dimly from the valley below.

The big guy was on his way.

"Move! Move! Move!"

They came to the little wooded promontory on top of a hill that formed a natural overlook above the valley. "Here!" The plan was to be there and be ready to go helicopter hunting by noon.

They had twenty minutes until show time.

The highlanders with the screens began binding them into the trees to form a hide for their gun position. The gun crew began setting up the weapon. One nice thing Red had discovered that Japanese Imperial armed forces had put antiaircraft sights on everything including their infantry rifles. But the majority of Japanese WWII machine guns required lubricated ammunition. The gun grease in storage had gone bad decades ago, and the gun oil had similarly congealed into black paste. Burdick didn't care to contemplate how long automatic fire could be sustained on coconut oil. He scowled ferociously.

His machine guns smelled like goddamn piña coladas.

"PIET! HOW CLOSE?"

Piet Dunkan crouched and examined a shrub. It would come thigh-high on a man, and there was a smear of blood on the leaf tips. He rubbed the blood between his fingers. It smeared across his fingertips easily. It had barely started to coagulate. He grinned as he attached a fresh rifle grenade to the muzzle of his BM-59 rifle. "Close, man. Real close."

Bryce Delvoix scanned the trees over the sights of his own rifle.

"Bryce!" The radio receiver earpiece crackled in Delvoix's ear. David Kiins was transmitting from the helicopter. "Movement! Two hundred meters from your position! Due west!"

"Affirmative!" He flipped the grenade sight a notch. The door guns of the Dauphin were already weaving threads of tracers down into the jungle. The rifle thudded against his shoulder as the antipersonnel grenade scudded out over the treetops. Dunkan's grenade flew a second later and the trees flashed yellow as they detonated one after the other. Delvoix checked the plastic-coated topo map taped to his thigh. His finger traced a line due west as shouted into his radio link.

"Kiins! They're heading for the foothills!" Dunkan began moving forward. Delvoix and his squad of Russians followed. "From there they can make their way up into the mountains! Get ahead of them! Drop a sniper team! We'll sweep them toward you!"

"Affirmative, Bryce!" The helicopter engine roared.

"Jensen! Your team! Sweep hard north. Flank them!"

The trap was closing.

Dunkan held up his fist and dropped to a crouch. There were more blood traces, and he was staring intently out into the bush. Delvoix and his team halted. Delvoix crept up beside his scout. "Where?"

Dunkan pointed.

There was a tiny movement in the underbrush. Delvoix saw a flash of dark skin. He raised his rifle to his shoulder and sighted. The silhouette of a man's head and shoulders were discernible through the leaves. He began squeezing his trigger.

A rifle cracked, and Delvoix blinked as blood sprayed into his eyes and his rifle was ripped from his hands. Dunkan whirled, leveling his weapon. The rifle in the trees cracked a second time, and Dunkan's throat burst. His head tilted over his shoulders at a horrific angle as only tendons held his shattered neck vertebrae together. His body collapsed like a puppet with its strings cut.

The Russians opened up with their rifles in a hailstorm of automatic fire in all directions.

Delvoix drew his .40-caliber Vektor pistol and began squeezing off rounds through the trees for his first target, but the black commando was already gone.

Delvoix lowered his pistol. The enemy had already moved on. Valdemar Solomon and his team came up on the run. "Jesus, man, your arm!" he said, startled.

Delvoix looked down. His rifle lay in the leaf mulch covered in blood. His hand still grasped the forestock. Delvoix checked his left arm and discovered there was little left but ragged flesh and shards of bone below the elbow joint.

BOLAN AND JAMES RAN for their lives.

The Executive Options men were good. Too good.

The enemy was on their trail, and above the jungle canopy the helicopter hovered like an Angel of Death. The canopy was thick, but the door gunners fired through it for effect. The helicopter had zoomed off. Bolan and James took the opportunity to sprint in an effort to put a cushion between themselves and their pursuers.

Rifle grenades boomed behind them, and they threw themselves down as yellow fire flashed and shrapnel hissed through the trees.

Their pursuers knew what they were doing, and they were not far behind.

"They're herding us, you know," James said. "And we're being flanked."

"They're leapfrogging guys ahead of us with the helicopter," Bolan replied.

The two men rose and continued their headlong run through the jungle. The land was rising toward the hills.

It was going to be very close.

THE HELICOPTER KNIFED across the jungle.

"There!" David Kiins pointed at a slight break in the canopy. A small pond and some rock formations made a dent in the jungle carpet. It was a perfect insertion point. "Pol! Put your team there! Bryce is driving them toward this spot!" Kiins looked over his shoulder. Just above the clearing were the foothills, and above them the path ran nearly straight up the mountain into the mist. They enemy barely needed herding.

The Dauphin was not a large transport and was flying on one engine. Kiins had several warning lights blinking on his instrument panel, but the rear cabin held a Russian sniper team reinforced with a light machine gunner and an extra spotter. Pol Thomas had a pair of canvas bags bulging with an assortment of antipersonnel mines and explosives. Once the snipers in the jungle were taken care of, all paths up the central mountain would be mapped and mined. By nightfall anything coming out of the highlands would face a gauntlet of fire and flying steel.

The pilot's eyes gleamed. One of his specialties was psychological warfare. The crates in the cabin held some of his own special toys. While Thomas and his team were mining the paths, Kiins had some surprises he intended on dropping onto the highland villages from above.

With the highlands bottled up, they could begin the final assault at their leisure.

Kiins slowed and orbited the clearing. "Ready ropes!"

The Russians slung fast rappel ropes out the cabin doors.

Thomas slung his bags and grabbed his rifle. He attached a grenade and then leaned out over the jungle and prepared to kick away. "Tell Bryce we will be in position in two minutes!"

"Affirmative!" Kiins jerked his thumb at the Russians. "Go! Go! Go!"

The four Russians deployed out the cabin doors.

Kiins rammed his throttles full forward into emergency war power. "Fuck!"

"Christ, man!" Thomas shouted. He clung to his rope with one hand and his heavy battle rifle thudded as it fired its grenade. He hung from his perch and kept his trigger down and burned a magazine on full auto. He roared at the door gunner. "There! There! Fire!"

Kiins swung his gaze toward the hilltop and spotted the target.

There was motion in the trees covering the hilltop. Strange motion. Portions of the jungle seemed to be falling away.

Thomas tossed in his empty rifle and swung back into the helicopter. He threw himself into the copilot seat with a smile. "Shit!"

"Fire!"

The helicopter filled the ring sight of the ancient machine gun. Red's fists clenched the twin pistol grips, and his thumbs shoved down on the paddle trigger. The weapon hammered to life in his hands. Flame spewed from the muzzle. Tracers drew smoking lines straight into the hovering aircraft. Off to one side Hitihiti cut loose with the light machine gun. The Ka'Kaio brothers knelt to either side, gritting their teeth and steadying the vibrating tripod of spears cradling the weapon.

The remaining half-dozen highlanders fired their rifles as fast as they could work the bolts. Some were shooting at the helicopter. Others were taking shots at the armed men descending out of it like spiders on the fast ropes. One of the spiders had stayed put and his remarkable return fire had blown off a highlander's head.

Tracers streamed as the door gunner began returning fire.

Red held down his trigger. Sh'sho knelt beside him in the loader's position, assisting the heavy brass strips of vintage ammunition into the feed ramp. The machine gun stuttered as it picked up each new strip and then sped up again to its firing rate of 450 rounds per minute.

Jon Ka'Kaio flew backward as tracers stitched him from crotch to collar. Hitihiti held his position and streamed fire back into the aircraft. It took but a few heartbeats to burn through his 30-round magazine. "Reload," he shouted.

Matt Ka'Kaio leaped up to take his dead brother's position as loader.

The helicopter jerked, and the men on the ropes plummeted to the rocks below.

Heat shimmered and rose from the cooling fins of Red's weapon and the stench of burning oil overpowered the smell of burned gunpowder. Red kept his sights dead on and poured lead into the helicopter. Black holes appeared in the fuselage and the windows cracked and spiderwebbed into opaqueness with bullet strikes. Red grinned savagely as he walked a burst across the open cabin door and the door gunner shuddered and collapsed in his chicken straps.

"Oh!" Sh'sho snatched his singed hands away from the feed ramp and dropped his stripper clip.

"Get on it!" Burdick screamed.

Smoke was pouring out of the action. Sh'sho scooped up the clip and shoved it into the smoldering, red-hot feed ramp. Red continued firing into the Dauphin. The helicopter dipped and skewed crazily over the clearing as the black smoke of burning oil belched from its exhaust.

Red held his trigger down. "Got…you…son of a bitch…"

Sh'sho snatched his hands away as a flame burst out of the feed ramp.

The coconut oil had ignited.

Burdick kept firing. The burning weapon continued to suck in the brass strips and spew rounds from the muzzle. The oiler cap blew off and a geyser of fire shot straight up out of the weapon. Red flinched and doggedly held on as burning oil spattered his forearms and face.

The nose of the smoking helicopter pointed straight at Red.

THE PILOT SQUEEZED his trigger.

The target below seemed to already be on fire. The rocket spewed flame under the weapons pylons as the electric igniters fired.

Kiins flinched as his windscreen pocked and cracked.

The helicopter lurched as bullets ripped into the cockpit. Kiins's finger unconsciously clamped on his trigger and his rockets salvoed off target in smoking ripples across the jungle. Thomas jerked and shuddered in the copilot seat as round after round hammered him into bloody oblivion. Blood and gore sprayed the interior of the besieged cockpit. Red lights glared across the instrument panel. Alarms chimed, and the single straining turbine screamed.

Kiins rammed his throttles forward again, but he was already losing power. Bullets continued to hammer the airframe as the helicopter spun out of control. The remaining door gunner screamed something in Russian.

The jungle loomed in a sickening green spin as the helicopter plummeted.

The pilot's vision went black as the helicopter broke its spine across the rock formations in the clearing.

THE EXECUTIONER RAN full tilt toward the smoke and fire ahead. James was right behind him. They hadn't been able to see it, but the entire western side of the island had to have heard the helicopter go down and the firecracker detonations of the rocket pods. They came to a clearing and found the smoking remains of the Dauphin.

A dead man lay charred in the copilot's seat. One door gunner hung shot to pieces in his chicken straps. The other's hips and lower torso were still attached to his harness. His upper half had been scraped off on the rocks.

The pilot was gone.

James knelt beside the smoldering wreck. "Tracks...and blood. The pilot walked out."

Bolan walked over to a heavy canvas bag that had been thrown clear and checked the contents. "Cal, check this."

James ambled over and peered inside. "Oh, yes."

The bag was a virtual candy store of antipersonnel unpleasantness.

Bolan slung the bag and they trotted up into the foothills. They'd done their damage for the day.

14

Church of England

"JESUS, MAN!" Rutgers shot up in his seat. David Kiins staggered into the command center. The right side of his face was a slag of blistered and burned flesh. He grabbed a beer from the bucket of ice in the corner. He pressed the sweating bottle against the ruins of his face and flopped on the couch. He looked at Rutgers accusingly.

"Heavy machine guns…" The pilot shook his head. "And just where the bloody hell did they get heavy machine guns, then?"

Rutgers raised an eyebrow at Gaz.

Gaz spit. "All heavy weapons are accounted for."

Kiins looked around blearily. The Menzies Mining office had been sandbagged and revetted with rammed earth and palm trunks inside and out. "I see you've redecorated."

Rutgers turned to the woman. "You sank Hitihiti's boat. They floated to shore, unarmed, did they not?"

"According to Gaz's report, they made their first attack against his men with rocks," she replied.

Rutgers dispatched a Russian to get a medic. "What can you report?"

"It was an ambush." The pilot winced as he pressed the

sweating bottle against his burned flesh. "Two support weapons that I could see. One light and one heavy. It happened very fast, but I could swear one of the weapons was already smoking, even burning, before I could fire back with rockets. There were numerous riflemen around them in the trees. The rate of fire was not high. I think bolt-action weapons. As the woman reported."

Rutgers shoved his laptop over to Gotwald. "Steppan, I want a list of all Japanese WWII small arms, up to light support and crew-served weapons issued in the Pacific Islands theater. Find a history of Japanese troop deployment on Pa'ahnui, anything regarding the conflict you can find."

"Right." Gotwald began hammering keys.

"Valdemar, find an interpreter, and then find me any islanders old enough to remember the fighting. I want accounts of who, what, where and when."

Valdemar slung his rifle and left.

Rutgers turned to the woman. "I need you to contact Craig. Tell him I need at least two helicopter gunships, four would be better."

"Craig is on his way." She checked her watch. "In fact he should be here within twenty-four hours. More helicopters will take time. We will have to either buy civilian helicopters in Australia and modify them, or somehow arrange to clandestinely get them on loan from the Papuan government."

Rutgers's face hardened. "If the Papuans want their billions out of this island, you tell them to send us some damned helicopters!"

Smakofani smiled. She did not like being yelled at by underlings. However, she approved of Rutgers's professionalism. "I will contact Craig immediately."

Rutgers stared at the map of Pa'ahnui that dominated the wall in front of the desk. "That will still probably be too long."

The woman held her phone in middial. "What do you propose?"

"We stick to the plan." Rutgers peered out the window. The panoramic view of the top office had been narrowed into a firing slit in the sandbags and heavy timber reinforcing the office. "We attack with everything. Full force."

Rutgers nodded to himself. "We attack tomorrow."

"WE ATTACK TONIGHT. With everything we got."

Truman Hitihiti's platinum blond eyebrows rose in alarm. "You fuckin' nuts, brah? We shot down their helicopter. Stopped them cold. They're licking their wounds, man."

"And we're licking ours." Red's hands and face were swathed in bandages. "We lost good men today. Half of the dozen highlanders I took down the mountain are wounded. Three are dead."

Sh'sho nodded. "We need time," he said.

"You're out of time." Bolan folded his arms across his chest. "Rutgers is going to attack tomorrow. He's going to march right up this mountain at dawn, and hellfire is coming with him. The paths up the mountain are narrow. If he's smart— and he is—he'll dismount his grenade launchers and blow the hell out of any resistance he finds on the way. We lost our heavy machine gun. The light is doubtful. So far you've been able to wipe out small incursions and probes, but the highlands aren't ready for a full-scale invasion. He'll take heavy casualties, but he won't care about expending pirates or Russian thugs. He wants to get this over with and go home. He's coming tomorrow, and he intends to win." Bolan looked around the circle of highlanders with their ancient weapons. "Wiping out poorly armed rebel movements is what he does best."

Sh'sho quietly translated what Bolan said to the rest of the war council. It was met with angry murmurs.

James looked resigned. "So you want to take C of E to-night?"

"I want to take the entire island," the Executioner said.

The men sitting in council sat straighter as Sh'sho trans-lated.

Bolan nodded. "Tonight Pa'ahnui is free."

The old men thumped their chests in agreement. They were sick of the interlopers on their island. This day they had scored a real victory. They were prepared to finish it.

"Send out runners. Through the highlands, through the valleys, along the coast. Send out the call for every man who can wield a spear."

Warriors ran from the longhouse.

Red turned to Bolan. "I have an idea."

15

"Gonna rip itself apart in three goes, brah." Hitihiti regarded the catapult with a mixture of awe and fear. "Probably gonna rip some arms off with it."

Bolan gazed at the monstrosity sitting in the middle of the village. The entire war council was assembled before it.

"Theoretically, what kind of range are we talking about?" he asked.

Inspector Filmoore chewed his stub of pencil. As the only artilleryman present, he had been elected siege engineer. "Dunno, mate. The math is pretty simple. But it's the variables that get dodgy. We're talking homemade rope, fresh cut trees, wet wood. No decent axle, hand release rather than a trigger. You might get two hundred yards, maybe, first go, then…"

It lay unspoken between them.

Then things would get dicey.

"So," Bolan said, "we're going to have some dispersion."

"Dispersion?" The inspector laughed. "You'll have quite a bit of that, no worries. And Truman? He's spot on. This machine'll rip itself apart right quick, and likely'll rip apart the lads working it when she goes."

Bolan didn't doubt it, but the more immediate question was range. Two hundred yards meant they would have to set up and throw practically from the tree line to hit targets in C of E. "Disassemble it and haul it down the mountain. Truman, build me another."

"Build you anoth—"He was reduced to Tongan expletives.

"You have three hours of light left. Make the best of them." Bolan turned to Sh'sho. "How many can we count on?"

Sh'sho puffed on his pipe. "From the coast, from the valley, from the highlands, maybe five hundred. Almost none with guns. They showing up with spears and machetes. They'll charge, once. After that…"

Bolan knew all too well what would happen if the charge failed. He glanced at Red. "You refilled your ranks?"

Red's blistered face grimaced. "Yeah, I picked up a dozen new boys. Gave them rifles and an hour of shooting and bayonet drill. You'll have your one hundred Spartans. Ready to charge the wire."

"How are we doing on those cannons?"

"I don't trust them. I don't like the look of the breeches at all. I think they're gonna blow themselves up after one or two shots. We haven't tested them, and we don't have crews trained yet."

"All right. Forget them. Give me a case of their ammo." Bolan turned to James. "You still got that jeep tucked away someplace?"

"Yeah, but it's unarmed."

A pair of highlanders manhandled a crate of 50 mm howitzer shells forward.

"It's armed now."

James sighed. "What are we going to use for a fuse?"

Bolan held up a pipe bomb.

"So who's leading the charge of the Light Brigade?" James asked, smiling.

Red rose to his feet. "I'll lead my men."

"No." Bolan shook his head. "You're our machine gunner. You're hanging back and shooting. The charge will depend on it."

Red flushed with sudden anger. " I trained them! I showed them which was the sharp end and told them what they were going to have to do. I'm not going to just pat them on the head and send them to their deaths!"

"I'll do it, brah."

The war council turned to look at Truman Hitihiti.

"You don't have to, Truman." Bolan measured the Tongan. "You and I are square. You've already gone way beyond the call of our contract. You didn't sign up for this war."

"Signing up now, brah." The Tongan eyes were deadly serious. "The islands, and I mean *all* the islands, been shit on for a century. I say fuck Menzies, fuck Craig and pardon me white man, but fuck you. This is an island thing."

The highland elders murmured angry agreement as Sh'sho translated.

The islanders were saying "no more."

Bolan nodded.

An ancient native approached Bolan and handed him an object. He held the spiral shell of a conch. Another was given to Sh'sho. The third was placed in Truman Hitihiti's hands.

They held the war horns of the highlands.

Pa'ahnui was going to war.

Si-Se and her sister brought Bolan another gift of battle.

The guardian skeleton they had found in the bunker had carried the weapon of his forefathers. The handle had rotted in his skeletal hands and the guard reduced to a disk of rust, but the blade had been salvaged. The split wooden sheath had been mended with bands of fiber.

Bolan drew the blade.

Half a century of disuse had left it pitted and deeply discolored, but the steel had been scoured and oiled and the thin hard arc of the edge gleamed from fresh sharpening. Bolan examined the edge and saw the wave of the *hamon*, the temper-line that ghosted along the edge like a cloud in the steel. This was a genuine sword of the samurai, made by traditional methods. The blade was undoubtedly centuries old.

It had undergone modification.

The rotted wood and rayskin hilt was gone. An intricately carved, fourteen-inch tiki of the Pa'ahnui god of war had replaced it. The idol had been split in two and then pegged and bound around the tang of the blade to form a new hilt. The rusted guard was gone and no effort had been made to replace it. The war god glared up at Bolan, eyes crossing at the blade protruding from his skull.

Si-Se and Hi'li watched Bolan's eyes, proud of their handiwork. The war council and the gathered highlanders seemed to hold their breath while Bolan examined the weapon.

The highlanders watched the warrior dance steel through the air.

The Executioner rammed the blade straight up into the dying sunlight and held it high overhead. It gleamed in a hard orange line with the sun and the volcano behind it. Bolan's blue eyes blazed. His voice shook the village square and bounced off the mountain behind them.

"Pa'ahnui!"

Rifles, spears, war clubs, machetes and fists shot skyward as the highlanders roared in response.

RUTGERS WENT OVER his plan a final time. It was simple, which was what he liked about it. The plan was to march up the mountain and kick the shit out of the rebels.

In the end, the rebels would have to make a stand, and when the attack began in earnest, the rebels would break.

Some would beat it into the bush, but with their villages taken, most would surrender. The rebels would be marched down to the coast and put into temporary camps. The Papuan government would relocate them. The mining operation would resume. Craig would make his millions. Rutgers sipped wine. And he would be the sole shareholder of Executive Options.

He looked at Gotwald, his second in command and nodded.

It was a good plan.

They would begin their attack at dawn.

A strange sound came droning through the firing slits. It came from the jungle. The long, sustained note was joined by a second and a third. Gotwald's hand went to his rifle. What is that? A horn?"

Rutgers shook his head. "The American is coming."

The firing slits lit up in orange flashes as explosions began rocking the town.

16

"LOCK AND LOAD." Truman Hitihiti spoke the words quietly to Matt Ka'Kaio. Ka'Kaio nodded and turned to the man next to him. The order was whispered down the line. Strict weapon discipline had been maintained all the way down the mountain. One accidental discharge in the dark would destroy the entire attack.

Hitihiti scanned the enemy defenses a final time. The three hard points were manned. He and Burdick's hundred trainees would be charging straight into interlocking lanes of machine-gun fire, but the enemy was clearly not expecting them. The men guarding the perimeter had night-vision scopes on their weapons, but for the most part their weapons were slung or rested on their thighs as they smoked and lounged around their revetments. Guard duty was the same the world over— deadly dull—and the men manning the Church of England's defenses were not waiting for an enemy attack. They were waiting for the final endless night of guard duty to be over so they could begin their own attack.

"Fix bayonets." Hitihiti whispered.

One hundred highlanders fixed razor-sharp steel to the ends of their rifles. The Tongan's massive hand curled around the conch and he raised the shell to his lips.

"Safeties off."

The huge shell vibrated in his hands, and the sound pealed forth and was matched by the other two conches in the trees.

Hitihiti burst from the trees tearing across the open sand of the killing zone, his bayonet pointed straight at the machine guns.

Red's men came screaming at his heels.

"FIRE!"

The straining highlander's let go of the ropes as the conches blared and the charge sounded from the trees.

"Clear!" Inspector Filmoore shouted.

The crew did not need to be told. They scrambled clear of the unstable siege engines as they went into motion. The two trebuchets let forth groaning sounds as timber ground against timber. The ropes creaked in protest. The throwing arms seemed to move in slow motion as the counterweights dropped. The sling ropes went taut and the sling of heavy fishing netting scraped along the rough plank.

The engine blocks crashed to the sand and the slings left the trough. The throwing arms swung vertical and the frame groaned in protest. The sling ropes kept going, their momentum moving them in an apocalyptic game of crack-the-whip. The slip rings slipped from the release pins and six 50 mm mortar bombs went airborne into the night.

"Reset!"

The crews leaped back in, hauling on ropes to lever the engine blocks back to the ready and pull the throwing arms back down.

"Prime!"

"Load!"

The loading crew positioned the slings in the trough and shoved bombs into netting.

Gunfire erupted along the perimeter. Seconds later the sky

flashed orange as high explosive shells detonated within the Church of England town square. The siege engine crews cheered raggedly.

"Ready!"

Both crew chiefs checked their slings. "Ready!"

"Fire!"

The counterweights crashed down and the throwing arms whipped up into the air.

CALVIN JAMES STOMPED the accelerator to the floor and popped in the electric cigarette lighter.

The jeep was so severely front loaded it was nearly impossible to steer. Two layers of sandbags had been lashed in front of the grille and piled three deep on top of the hood. The ancient leaf-spring suspension was nearly flattened by the load. However, all that was required was that the vehicle survive its short run.

Flares sailed into the sky from the strong points along the trench. A machine gun opened up and was immediately silenced as a rifle cracked somewhere in the trees behind. Mack Bolan was an angel on their shoulders as the attack commenced. Alarm whistles along the perimeter of the town sounded. Another machine gun opened fire, and Red hammered tracers into it from the trees. The area lit up with the detonations of the inspector's 50 mm mortar bombs.

In the back bed of the jeep was a loose pile of one dozen 70 mm howitzer rounds. Hunched down, James reached between the seats and picked up a pipe bomb as the cigarette lighter popped out, its coils bright orange with heat. He touched the glowing coil to the fuse of the pipe bomb. Sparks flew as the fuse caught.

James flipped the sizzling pipe bomb onto the pile of cannon rounds and took the steering wheel in both hands.

Sand flew and spurted across the hood as bullets ripped into the sandbag cocoon defending the engine. The jeep lurched as the right front tire exploded and rubber shredded as James kept the hammer down. Rifle fire was pouring into his vehicle, taking heat off the highlanders. James risked a look over the hood.

The little sandbag castle forming the outer gate of the perimeter was less than twenty-five yards away.

James threw himself from the jeep.

He soared through space as tracers streaked around him. He watched as the vehicle plowed into the side of the gate and bounced to a stop. James hit the lip of the entrenchment with bone-jarring impact. Barbed wire ripped into his flesh. The sand slid beneath him, and he rolled out of control. Bamboo pungee sticks snapped underneath him as he tumbled but he was rolling with the grain. He collapsed in a heap at the bottom of the trench.

The world above him went orange.

THE EXECUTIONER sighted and fired. The light machine gun fell silent for the third time. He furiously worked his smoking bolt and chambered another round. He raised his sights to the flame stuttering from the top of the church steeple. The gunner's chest was smashed in. Bolan lowered his sights and swept the perimeter. The charging highlanders were blocking his line of fire. They had taken casualties, but they were going to reach the wire. Bolan set aside his rifle and blew two blasts on his conch.

Sh'sho's conch blasted twice in answer.

Bolan drew his Astra pistol and flicked off the safety. The samurai sword was unsheathed. He held the blade high like a banner and charged forward.

The five hundred islanders of the second wave came howl-

ing out of the trees brandishing spears, war clubs and machetes. Bolan led them as Hitihiti's troops began shooting.

As Bolan charged, he saw the red taillights of the jeep as
it tore forward and James bailed out.

The roar of the charging natives rose to a scream of venge-
ance as the car bomb exploded.

The second wave rolled across no-man's land.

17

"We've lost the perimeter." Delvoix tossed aside his binoculars and drew his .40-caliber Vektor. "They'll be massing for their next attack."

"Jensen's dead." Kiins's eyes glared out of his burned face as he scanned the trench.

Rutgers checked the loads in his rifle. "Where the hell is Gaz?"

Gotwald was stuffing his pockets with grenades. "He and his remaining men are hiding in the barracks. I believe Gabriello's men are in the warehouse."

"Is there anyone left alive on the perimeter?" Rutgers asked.

"No." Gotwald held his headphones to one ear. The frantic calls for assistance had ceased. The com link was silent. "I don't think the enemy is taking prisoners."

"Fine, then." Rutgers fixed his bayonet. "We break for the boat."

Lizabet Smakofani sat drinking South African sauvignon blanc. Her arm was in a sling. The Drotik machine pistol lay in her lap. "What about Gabriello and Gaz?" She was smirking slightly as she inquired. "And their men?"

"Fuck them," Rutgers said.

She smiled.

Gotwald froze in place at the radio set.

"What is it?" Rutgers demanded to know.

Gotwald stared at the dial. "A communication. Coming across the Russian individual radio-link frequency. Someone wishing to speak to Commander Rutgers."

Rutgers frowned. "Put it on speaker."

Gotwald clicked a button and Rutgers spoke. "To whom am I speaking?"

"Your opponent." The voice that spoke back was as cold as the bottom of a freshly dug grave. "You're finished. Surrender, immediately."

"Surrender?" Rutgers snorted with a great deal more derision than he felt. "What are you going to do, lead a bayonet charge against fortified buildings?"

"Yes."

The command center was silent for a moment.

"Listen very carefully, Commander," the voice said.

"Listen to what?" the Dutchman replied, seething.

"To the drums."

Silence reigned once more. The mortars had stopped falling. The natives had stopped howling and shooting. It took a moment, but the throbbing sound was suddenly clear.

War drums.

"We hit your trench with six hundred. The drums are talking across the island and the word of our victory is out. Scores of men are showing up every minute. The highlanders are coming down from the mountains. By dawn we'll be thousands."

"Thousands with machetes and pointed sticks!" Rutgers said.

"I have 150 rifles, and I just picked up about forty more. I also just picked up four light machine guns and a 40 mm automatic grenade launcher. I have your trench line and every weapon that was on it. I believe your support weapons are still mounted on your jeeps."

Rutgers glared out the window. The jeeps were riddled with bullets, as were the bodies of about two dozen men who had tried to reach them.

His opponent read his mind. "Try to get them, Rutgers. I dare you. And before you try to shoot your way out and make for the pier, let me inform you that the pier is on fire. Your boat is on fire, too, and appears to be floating toward New Zealand."

Delvoix stared out across the water and nodded in confirmation.

"You have thirty seconds to comply. Throw down your weapons and come out into the town square with your hands up and kneel. If you fail to do so, I will recommence the attack."

"You come, boy!" Delvoix shouted in a cold rage. "You come, and you see what happens!"

"Rutgers." The voice was as compassionless as fate. "You're a professional. You know you've lost. There's been enough killing. End this."

Rutgers let out a long slow breath. His voice was dead as he uttered words he'd once sworn he die before saying. "What are your terms?"

"No terms. Your surrender will be unconditional and immediate."

"Fuck you, boyo!" Delvoix leaned into the microphone. "You see what happens."

"Right now I have control," the voice continued speaking. "But you know what Gaz and his men have done here, and every native on this island knows what Craig intends to do to the land. The people here have been looted, raped and savaged, and they've had enough. God help you if you make us assault. I won't be able to control them. Anyone taken alive will pay the price."

Rutgers made another motion and Gotwald squelched the speaker. Rutgers looked at his second in command. Gotwald shook his head in defeat. "There's but five of us left, Commander."

Rutgers nodded. "Kiins?"

Kiins would not meet his eyes.

"Bryce."

Bryce was staring at his stump. It was bleeding again.

"Bryce?"

"Fuck, Craig. Fuck this island." Delvoix threw his pistol on the table in disgust. "And fuck you for bringing us here, then."

Rutgers turned to the woman. "I'm going to surrender. I believe what this man says, but I am not sure if he can stop reprisals, particularly against Gaz and his men. I'm going to try and surrender directly to him and distance ourselves from Gaz and Gabriello. Stay close to us. I will try to protect you—"

"Hold that thought, Commander." She clicked open her phone and punched a button. She cocked her head and listened for a moment. "Really? Yes, that is the situation. No, I want to do it. Very good Mr. Craig." She clicked the phone shut. "You are not authorized to surrender."

"Not…authorized?" Rutgers stared. "But—"

"Get Gaz and Gabriello on the radio." The woman nodded as she rose from the couch. "We counterattack immediately."

"THE LINE'S DEAD." The Executioner kept his eyes on the fortified Menzies building. "He hasn't responded."

"That's messed up. Rutgers is a pro." James spit in the sand. "I don't like it."

"Neither do I." Bolan turned to Sh'sho. "Send a runner to Filmoore. Tell him to resume shelling the village."

"What in the blue hell?" Red was staring through a captured pair of binoculars.

Bolan raised his commandeered rifle and scanned through the optics. Something was coming across the water, and it was huge. "Red, you're a boating man, how big?"

"Eighty meters, at least. Big, real big." Red shook his head respectfully. "He's got three hulls. Goddamn! That's *The Triple Witch!* Craig's boat. I've read about it. Make that a hundred meters. It's the only one of its kind."

"He's coming in fast," Bolan said.

"He's coming in real fast. He's going to run her aground if he doesn't—"

The Triple Witch ground to a halt in the sand. The prows of the two outlying hulls split open like clamshells.

"We're about to be counterattacked!" Bolan's voice boomed along the line. "Counterattack coming! Get ready!"

Red dropped down behind one of the light machine guns.

A pair of Land Rover Defenders rolled down the ramp of each open hull. Each had a shielded weapon system mounted on its roof. The air thudded with the sound of rotors and a helicopter rose up from behind the trimaran's bridge. One of the vehicles drove up to the Menzies building and someone dashed out the door and dived into the waiting vehicle.

It was Juliet Thomas.

Russians and pirates began deploying out of the buildings in a mob.

"Fire!" Bolan commanded.

Rifles opened up all along the trench line, followed by the light machine guns. The Land Rovers drove straight into the fusillade. Sparks flew from the car bodies. The vehicles had armored body panels and windshields. It would take antitank weapons to stop them.

Bolan and the natives of Pa'ahnui were fresh out that morning.

Truman Hitihiti charged from the trench line with twenty highlanders behind him. Each man carried lit pipe bombs.

The two Land Rovers stopped. Their chassis rocked as every highlander with a firearm hammered them. Bolan's stomach sank as he heard the high pitched whine of motors powering up.

The Land Rovers suddenly began to return fire.

Tracers began streaming from the roof-mounted machine guns. Craig had General Electric "Six-Packs" mounted on his vehicles. Their rate of fire climbed from a stuttering roar to a sound like the continuing tearing of canvas.

Red fired back with little effect. His captured PK light machine gun would do six hundred rounds per minute.

The motorized Gatlings on the Land Rovers were firing at six thousand.

The tracers blurred into continuous laserlike lines as the Six-Packs swept the trench line with surgical precision.

Bolan fired his rifle dry and threw himself down as one of the weapons played over his position.

The islanders had been utterly suppressed. Anyone who hadn't been shredded in the opening salvo was hugging sand.

The Land Rovers were moving forward again. Bolan risked a squint over a sandbag. The Russians and the pirates were following behind the vehicles in a skirmishing line, firing bursts from their rifles as they came.

The helicopter thundered over their position and arrowed for the tree line.

James had picked up a fallen Arisaka rifle. He glanced back as he pressed in a fresh five-round clip. "He's going after our catapults."

Bolan gazed at the killing ground between the trench and trees. "Then he'll be back for us."

"This is so fucked." Red stared over the sights of his light machine gun helplessly. "We had them. We goddamn had them."

"Sho, Calvin. We have only a few seconds. This is your revolution. How do you want to play it?"

Sh'sho ran his eye down the trench line. He took in the shattered corpses of the dead and the cringing postures of the wounded. To charge would be suicide. The only question was whether or not to die fighting. Tears of rage and frustration spilled down his cheeks. "We must save my people. We must save as many as we can."

Bolan spoke into the Russian tactical radio. "Rutgers, hold your fire. We are prepared to surrender. I told you before to end it. End it now. You've won."

There was nothing but silence across the link.

"We will throw down our weapons. We will dismantle the defenses in the Highlands and lead your men to all caches of weapons. All we ask is that there be no reprisals against the villages."

Rutgers spoke across the link. "I regret to inform you I cannot accept your surrender. I am no longer in command of this operation."

Calvin, Sh'sho and Red were all wearing Russian com links stripped from the dead. They stared at one another as a third voice spoke genially across the link.

"I gather I'm speaking to my...opponent?"

Bolan could hear the sound of rotor noise across the radio. Craig was in the helicopter.

"I'll accept your surrender. Have your men throw down their weapons, and proceed out of the entrenchment, single file, hands up in the air, and march down to the beach. Leave your wounded. They will be attended to. All nonnatives will be debriefed and then immediately deported to the Solomon Islands. I will meet with the Island's native leaders to resolve this situation. I have the legal right to develop the mineral resources of this island, but I do not want any further debacle. Neither does the Papuan government. I am losing money by the minute, and I am prepared, within limits, to renegotiate."

Sh'sho grimaced. "Can we trust him?"

Red grunted unhappily. "I think we can trust him to line us up and shoot us in the surf with those goddamn motorized zip guns of his."

"I'm with Red on this one." James shook his head. "This guy let Gaz off the leash and didn't give a shit. He doesn't give a shit now."

Bolan's instincts spoke to him. Craig was enjoying this.

He spoke into his mike. "We are prepared to surrender. Let me inform my commanders."

"You have exactly one minute."

Bolan squelched his mike. "Sho, send word down the line. Get ready to run for the trees. Tell Truman and whoever he has left that we are fighting a delaying action as long as we can."

Bolan and Sh'sho took their conches from the woven bags around their necks and blew the three short, hard blasts that signaled the retreat. Red's machine gun ripped into life as he roared at the highlanders around him. "Go! Go! Go!"

Stephen Craig's voice spoke in Bolan's ear. "Interesting."

The natives scrambled down into the trench and clawed their way back up to the killing zone between themselves and the safety of the trees. Hitihiti and his surviving troops stood their ground. Fuses hissed as they lit pipe bombs and hurled them into the oncoming enemy wave.

The miniguns resumed spewing their swarms of lead instantly.

A native with a lit Molotov cocktail in each hand ignited as he was caught in the motorized fusillade. The heads of two more exploded as they lunged for the light machine guns.

Hitihiti stood and hurled a firebomb with javelin-like accuracy. It corkscrewed through the air and erupted into flame across the armored glass of a Land Rover's windshield. Flaming objects flew in a sudden rain as the islanders blindly lobbed their homemade bombs over the battlements. Russians and pirates threw themselves down and fired their rifles as pipe bombs burst into lethal fragments and Molotov's littered the ground with pools of fire.

Bolan ran down the trench line. He threw aside his rifle and dived for the spade grips of one of the abandoned MK 19 automatic grenade launchers. He spun the weapon around on its mount. He aimed at one of the oncoming Land Rovers and raised the ring sights to the strobing fire coming from the weapon mounted on the roof of the vehicle. The grenade launcher was loaded with antipersonnel fragmentation rounds, exactly the sort of weapon the Land Rover's armored glass, body panels and run-flat tires were designed to defeat. A steel shield protected the gun on top, but the weapon had to protrude its barrels through the slit and aim with its optics.

Bolan rammed his selector switch to semiauto and fired.

He placed one shot per second directly into the muzzleblast of the minigun. Sparks shrieked on the metal shield as hundreds of steel fragments hissed out from the detonating grenades. Bolan continued to light up the weapon emplacement even as it swung its six barrels in his direction. He was rewarded as the muzzles of the minigun dipped and tilted skyward as the gunner manning the weapon took hits.

Bolan's weapon locked on empty as he expended his belt of ammo.

He threw himself aside as the second Land Rover opened

fire on him. The MK 19 lit up like a Christmas tree and sagged in its mount as several hundred rounds struck it. Bolan belly crawled for a fallen rifle. He looked back and saw most of the natives had made it back to the shelter of the trees.

Above the jungle the orbiting helicopter lit up as the minigun under its weapons pylons began drawing solid lines of death into the jungle below. The tree line lit up orange with detonation after detonation as the catapults and their piles of mortar bombs were caught in the murderous firestorm.

Bolan fired his rifle between a pair of ruptured sandbags and put down a pair of advancing pirates.

The siege was over. They were back to a guerrilla campaign. That was if there were anything left of the guerrillas by dawn. The helicopter was running without lights. It was very clear it was hunting targets with infrared optics.

Bolan saw Calvin James down in the trench. The ex-SEAL lit a pipe bomb and tossed it over the shredded sandbags he was using for cover. "Calvin!" Bolan shouted above the gunfire. "Get out of here!"

"Both of you get out of here!" Hitihiti's voice roared. Blood was running down his face. He crouched by the shattered remnants of the blockhouse cradling a Russian light machine gun. He glared at Bolan. "Go find that sniper rifle, brah! This ain't over!" He rose and began firing his weapon.

"Pa'ahnui!" Hitihiti's men cheered raggedly as they raised their weapons and fired.

Bamboo stakes snapped beneath Bolan's boots as he leaped to the bottom of the moat. Sand shifted beneath his feet as he scrambled his way up and over the top. He made a beeline for the spot where he had left the Arisaka sniper rifle. Behind him Hitihiti's conch blasted three times signaling final retreat. It was most likely too late. Bolan could hear shouts in Russian and Tagalog and the rifle fire was almost constant as they stormed the perimeter.

James sprinted at Bolan's side. "Where's Red?"

"Don't know!"

Bolan ran past a forked tree and scooped up his rifle and his bandolier of ammo.

Stephen Craig spoke smugly across the link. "I...see... you..."

"Break!" Bolan shouted.

Rotors whipped the trees as the helicopter swooped down. Bolan broke left and James broke right.

Red tracers tore through the tree canopy as the twin miniguns burned into life.

18

The sun was coming up. The Executioner could still hear the helicopter patrolling inland to the north. The sound was occasionally punctuated by bursts from the miniguns. He tore away the sleeve of his T-shirt and turned his attention to his optics. His weapon was filthy after a night of playing hide-and-seek with the helicopter. He spit on the glass of the power scope and gingerly removed sand and dirt from the lenses.

Stephen Craig spoke across the line. "Hey, asshole."

Bolan had been monitoring the frequency all night.

It had been very busy, but most of the brief communications had been in Russian or Tagalog. Craig would know he was being monitored and would be using interpreters so the opposition could not understand his battle commands.

Bolan had been tempted to use the link to contact Calvin James, Red or Sh'sho, but he knew the enemy would have the ability to triangulate. Listening passively had been the only option. Now Craig was speaking to him directly.

"Listen, shithead, I know you're not going to answer, just listen real carefully."

Bolan listened.

"This island? It's mine. Ilya Gaz? He's a saint compared to me, and what I'm going to do here."

Bolan didn't doubt it.

"I suggest you surrender while you can. You intrigue me just enough that you might just walk out of this. Who knows, possibly with a job."

Bolan nodded. His every instinct told him that on the other end of the link Craig was smiling.

"Oh, you know something else? I have your buddy, Truman."

Bolan's blood went cold.

"Truman's not doing too well. But I also have that giant redheaded fuck of yours."

Bolan considered his bandolier of ammunition. He had exactly twenty-seven rounds for the Arisaka, but he knew where he could get more.

Craig seemed to read his mind.

"Just an FYI, I'm going to feed them to my dogs, today, around noon."

Bolan glanced at the rising sun. It was around eight o'clock. There wasn't going to be time to climb up the mountain and get more ammo. Bolan stuck his hand into the wet jungle soil and began smearing himself with mud.

19

Bolan's blue eyes filled with rage as he stared through his riflescope. His knuckles whitened around the rifle's grips.

Truman Hitihiti had been crucified.

A dozen men from Craig's security team stood in an arc around the execution ground. They wore their black raid suits and armor and had 100-round drums loaded in their G-36 rifles. Their bayonets were fixed. The two Land Rovers were parked off to either side. Those Russians and pirates not on guard duty were gathered around in clumps to watch the proceedings. Gaz and Gabriello were both in attendance.

Rutgers and any of his surviving men were nowhere in sight. Neither were Craig or the woman. There was no sign of Red.

Bolan scanned the scene of the previous night's battle. The perimeter had been rearmed and remanned. The shattered blockhouse and gate had been shored up with sandbags and palm trunks. Bulldozers had been pulled out of the equipment park at the edge of the village.

Bolan scanned for Craig.

"Hey, shithead." The billionaire psychopath's voice chimed into Bolan's earpiece right on cue. "You out there?"

Bolan ran his sights over the Menzies Mining Office, but he could make out nothing past the firing slits.

"Here, let's have a little three-way chat."

Your redheaded buddy is here with us. Hey copper-top, say something charming to your little pal."

There was a gurgle and Red croaked across the link. "Striker, you listening?"

Bolan listened.

"Fuck Craig. I can't reach him with my hands tied. So you fuck him."

Red grunted and there were sounds like a butcher trying to tenderize a side of beef.

Bolan whipped his scope around. The Land Rover on the right was rocking slightly on its chassis. Red was getting pounded, but he had just announced his location—and Craig's. What to do with the information was a problem. The Land Rover's windshield was tinted, and armored. Even if he could put a bullet through it he didn't know who was in which seat.

"Charming asshole, isn't he?" Craig was enjoying himself thoroughly. "But of course that's why you brought him in. I commend his toughness and his loyalty. It's a damn shame." Craig paused for dramatic effect. "Did I mention I was going to feed him to my dogs?"

The driver's door on the Land Rover to the left opened. One of Craig's hardmen emerged and went around to the back. He opened up the tailgate and four immense, black mastiffs leapt to the sand.

Craig laughed.

Bolan flicked off the Arisaka rifle's safety.

The right-hand rear passenger door of the Land Rover on the right kicked open. The four mastiffs looked at their master. Bolan's eyes narrowed. Craig was in the right-hand passenger seat. He calculated the angles. All he had was the front of the Rover and a very partial view of the front passenger window.

He didn't have a shot.

Bolan checked the palm trees by the beach. Their fronds sagged motionless in the midday heat. There was no wind. Red would be in the front passenger seat shackled and being covered by the driver. Craig would be in back, probably right behind Red. To hit Craig he would have to try to go through the passenger window. That was a glancing shot, with a light, 6 mm bullet against armored glass with no positive visual on the target behind it.

At eight hundred yards.

It was no shot at all.

There was no choice.

No choice at all.

"Bastard!" Red screamed. "You goddamn bastard! I'll kill—"

Red's pounding inside the Rover resumed.

"Fuck you." Red sat in the passenger seat of the Land Rover and bled. His hands were tied behind his back. He threw back his head and roared in bitter contempt.

Craig leaned forward and spoke in Red's ear. "Say goodbye," he whispered.

Red snapped his head back with all of his strength. Pain knifed through his cranium as his occipital lobe made brutal contact with Stephen Craig's face. Red ignored his blurring vision and swung his forehead around in a vicious arc and slammed it into the skull of the hardman behind the steering wheel. Stars exploded across his vision as the thin bone of the man's temple cracked with the impact.

The former Marine heaved his entire body against his bonds. He groaned in an agony of effort as his wrists torqued. His trapezius muscles crowded against his skull as every muscle in his body heaved in concert. Blood flew from his wrists as the rope snapped.

"Fuck you!" Red's mangled face was hideous as it twisted in suicidal triumph. He pumped his fist three times into the cracked skull of the hardman to keep him down and then reached across him to fling open the driver's door. Red shoved him out to the sand and slid behind the wheel.

Craig groaned behind Red in the back seat. Red distinctly heard the sound of a holster unsnapping. "That was a—"

"Didn't you hear me?" Red shoved the Land Rover into first and stomped on the accelerator. "I said fuck you."

Red braced himself against the wheel with both hands as the vehicle flew forward. The Land Rover roared past Truman's sagging corpse and rammed straight into the other Land Rover broadside.

Craig flew over the front passenger seat and hit the windshield before bouncing back again.

Red's nose broke a second time as his face bounced against the steering wheel. The bones in his left hand broke against the dash. Burdick sat up blinking and sneezing blood. He noted Craig's pistol now languishing in the passenger seat and took it in his right hand.

"Hey, Craig, fuck you and die."

The rear passenger door flung open as Red aimed the pistol past the headrest with a shaky hand. The pistol barked three times in rapid succession as Craig slithered to the sand and kicked the door shut behind him.

Red dropped the pistol back into the bucket seat and rammed the Land Rover into reverse as bullets began striking it from all sides. He hoped to feel the speed bump of Craig's body as he ran him over, but all his tires grabbed was sand. Red threw the vehicle into first. The windows and body panels of the vehicle ticked and popped as if it were caught in a hailstorm. Craig's hardmen, the Russians and the pirates were all spraying their weapons at the vehicle at point-blank range, but the Land Rover Defender's VIP protection armor held.

"Gotta get me one of these…" Red steered with his elbow as he put on his seat belt.

Burdick drove up the beach onto the single road of the town and headed for the perimeter gate. Red knew the VIP armor was rated against rifle fire, but he wondered exactly how much rifle fire it could take before it buckled. This wasn't a single assassination attempt or ambush. He was running a goddamn gauntlet.

The perimeter weapons swung around on their mounts and began hammering him on his approach. The Land Rover lurched and shuddered as 40 mm frags began detonating against its armored skin. The windshield veined and cracked as the light machine guns snarled. Red flinched as a neat bullet hole appeared in the windshield and the passenger-seat headrest exploded. A second, third and fourth bullet hole appeared in rapid succession. The armored glass began making tinking and squeaking noises as cracks shot through it from end to end.

Red rammed through the gate.

The windshield went opaque sagged out of its frame and flopped across Red and the front seats like a giant, jagged sheet of pizza dough. The perimeter weapons swung back around and hammered the Rover's rear door and window. The considerable, cutting weight of the collapsed ballistic-grade glass prevented Red from shifting. The engine's roar rose to a howl as he redlined it in second gear for the tree line.

The machine gun and grenade fire tapered off as he passed under the cover of the jungle canopy. Red braked as something stepped out of the trees and onto the road. It appeared to be a creature made of mud, carrying an Imperial Japanese Type 98 sniper rifle. Red pulled over and rolled down his window.

The mud man leaned on his rifle wearily.

Red grinned through the mashed meat of his face. "Hey, sailor, want a date?"

20

"Nice ride, Striker." Calvin James stood by the side of the road, leaning on a spear and eyeing the Land Rover. Its bullet-riddled exterior looked like a wasp's nest on wheels. The front bumper was crumpled. The engine hiccuped and the idle was distinctly wrong. Wisps of steam leaked out from under the folded hood.

Red spit some blood. "It came with extras."

"Like?"

"Like a GE Six-Pack." Red glanced at the roof-mounted weapon over his head and nodded toward the cargo compartment in back. "And two extra 1000-round ammo packs."

There had also been a pair of G-36 rifles racked in the back with ammo. "Get in, get yourself a rifle." Bolan glanced at his watch. "Let's do some distance and then get off the road."

James eyed the swollen sausages that Red had for fingers on his left hand. "Why don't you let me drive."

"I could use a rest." Red clambered out and got in back. He didn't sit down however. He stood up in the gunner's turret and got behind the Six-Pack.

James shoved the beat up Land Rover into gear. "Where to?"

"They'll most likely start their search in a straight line for the highlands. Let's drive along the coast for a bit, then hide this rig under the trees."

"Right." He headed for the beach road. "I can't believe we lost Truman."

Red rumbled thoughtfully from the gun position above. "He was a good man."

"He was a smuggler. Guns and drugs, and he didn't care. He wasn't pedaling or pushing on the street, but he knew what kind of misery he was carrying."

"Jesus, Striker. He still didn't deserve to die like—"

"He fell going forward, and he died defiant," Bolan said thoughtfully. "Before this is over, we're probably going to envy him. It's only going to get worse from here."

Red considered how he'd spent the morning strapped to a fishing chair and was silent.

James nodded. The situation was grim. "So how do you want to play it?"

"You had some of your people stash supplies down here in the jungle, didn't you?" Bolan asked.

"Yeah, but it's all ammo and munitions. Every gun we had was spoken for, and the natives have scattered in all directions. We need to find someone who can drum-talk and have them put out the call to regroup."

"We do that tonight. We have plenty of guns here in the Rover. It's the munitions I want."

"That's gonna be maybe two or three cases of mortar bombs, and we're not going to be building catapults anytime soon."

"Mortar bombs are exactly what I want."

James had heard that speculative tone in Bolan's voice more times than he cared to remember. The big guy was up to something, no doubt dangerous. "What have you got in mind?"

"We're going to go fishing."

"What are we fishing for?"

"Helicopters."

The Triple Witch

RUTGERS GAVE HIS REPORT. "One hundred and thirty-five effectives. Not counting your private security force."

Craig steepled his fingers on the table.

"The Russians are down to about fifty men still in fighting condition. The Filipinos about seventy-five." Rutgers made no attempt to hide his disdain. "Though I have my doubts about their effectiveness in infantry combat. We are down to three operational gun jeeps, none of which are in any kind of condition for sustained duty. The remaining Land Rover is running, but the driver's-side body panels are buckled, and I would no longer rate it as bulletproof."

Craig peered intently at the map of the island on the wall of the office. Rutgers wasn't telling him anything he didn't already know. The fact was there were thousands of natives on the island, and he no longer had the men or vehicles to project force effectively. Given another day or two the natives would remass and attack again. They were probably feverishly building new catapults while Rutgers reported.

Craig stared at the map.

He really didn't care about the island or the wealth that lay underneath it. What really mattered to him was the defiance that he'd been shown. He wanted the natives brutally conquered. Given his druthers, he'd like them exterminated like vermin.

Extermination.

That was the key.

Rutgers trailed off as Craig flipped open his phone. Craig punched a button and spoke to his communications man on the bridge. "Patch me through to Hong Kong on the secure line."

"Yes, Mr. Craig."

The phone rang once and a voice with a slight, undecipherable accent answered. "Hello, Mr. Craig. I am pleased to hear from you. You have considered my proposition?"

"Yes, how soon can you get here?"

"Well, by happy coincidence I happen to be in the Coral Sea. I can make landfall on Pa'ahnui within forty-eight hours."

The happy coincidence meant the bastard had operatives on the island and was aware of the exact situation, Craig thought. That didn't matter. "You have what we discussed?"

"Indeed, everything is accounted for."

"I would like to make one change."

"Oh?"

Rutgers's eyes went wide as he listened to what Stephen Craig wanted.

"I'll see you in forty-eight hours." Craig clicked off the phone and turned to Rutgers. "I want strafing runs on the highland villages. I want the rebels kept off balance."

Rutgers scowled. "I will see to it."

TRACERS STREAKED DOWN in twin red lines. The natives below erupted into red ribbons. Kiins took his finger off the trigger as the two Pa'ahnuian riflemen collapsed in heaps. He orbited the clearing in a search pattern. "You see anymore, then?"

Craig's head security man sat in the copilot's seat sweeping the green carpet below with his binoculars. "No."

"Val?"

Valdemar Solomon's black eyes scrutinized the jungle floor through the optical sight of his M-76 semiautomatic sniper rifle. "It looks safe."

Kiins dropped the helicopter into the clearing, and one of the security men jumped from the back and collected the rifles from the dead natives. The radio crackled and Gotwald spoke. "Kiins! The Land Rover has been sighted near the village on the northern coast!"

Kiins checked the map in the clear plastic pocket of his flight suit. "I can be there in five minutes."

"Advise caution, the Land Rover is armed with a minigun, and according to the report has at least two spare ammo packs."

"Acknowledged." Kiins wasn't too worried. Craig did nothing halfway. The Kawasaki BK 117 helicopter had every amenity, including a custom armor package that would withstand shell splinters and direct hits from up to .30-caliber small-arms fire. The Six-Pack on the stolen Land Rover was .22-caliber, and its bullets far too light to do any real damage. Still, at a thousand rounds per minute it might just be able to batter a hole somewhere in the fuselage.

Kiins had no intention of sitting in the American's sights for that long.

The helicopter rose from the clearing and dipped its nose toward the coast. The jungle swept by below and the ocean gleamed ahead.

Nothing on the island was very far from anything else. It was the endless wall of nearly vertical terrain that made ground operations difficult. Kiins banked over the village and swung west along the road. "Everyone, keep an eye out, we're getting close."

The helicopter suddenly vibrated as the left side of the cockpit took two hundred rounds in the space of two seconds. Kiins rammed his throttles forward and dived for the deck.

"I think we found them," Solomon said. He flicked the safety off his rifle.

Another burst hit the helicopter.

"There!" The security man pointed down, but Kiins had already seen the streaking tracer lines and followed them to their point of origin in the jungle below. There was a clearing just off the road. The Land Rover was at one edge of the clearing with brush piled on it. It was ideally situated to ambush vehicles coming in either direction. Kiins swung the helicopter's armored nose and put his sights on the vehicle.

The black commando was behind the armored shield. He desperately held his trigger down and spewed fire up at the aircraft. His bullets rattled and broke apart against the armored glass.

Kiins returned fire.

He squeezed his trigger and held it down for five seconds. The Land Rover's brush camouflage disintegrated and the vehicle nearly disappeared beneath the showering sparks as one thousand rounds impacted it. But the miniguns would not penetrate its panels. However, anyone standing up in the firing roof would be slaughtered.

Kiins released his trigger.

The armored firing cupola on the Land Rover seemed to be abandoned. The gunner was either dead or had prudently ducked inside the vehicle. Kiins could not see through the tinted windows, but neither did he see any blood or body parts littering the roof. "He's holed up inside."

The security man clicked a high-explosive armor-piercing grenade on the end of his rifle. "Not for long," he said.

Kiins kept his gun sight on the vehicle as he landed the helicopter. "Be careful, there may be more of them hidden in the trees—"

The rear door of the Land Rover burst open and the black commando lunged out and sprinted across the clearing, spraying the helicopter with rifle fire to cover himself.

"Bastard!" Solomon kicked open the copilot door. The high-powered rifle bucked in his hands. "Come on!"

The American was already in the trees.

The six-man Craig Consortium security team deployed from the helicopter in two-man teams to hold the perimeter. Solomon and the security leader crouched beneath the rotors and moved toward the abandoned vehicle. They leveled their weapons and peered cautiously through the open door.

There was no one inside.

The security man frowned. "It was the redheaded asshole who stole the vehicle."

"But it was the black guy we drove out now," Solomon replied.

"The big man had been tortured. He may be too injured to continue fighting."

Solomon grunted. He had seen the big redhead. He suspected he would have to be dead to be unable to fight. He was close. Solomon could smell him. He noted a pair of wooden crates in the back cargo area. One had its lid open. He put a hand on the other man's shoulder. "Touch nothing."

"What is it?"

Solomon looked again. One of the two crates had its lid pried off. The cylindrical objects had brass fittings that were green with age, but he recognized them for what they were.

They were mortar bombs. Two dozen of them counting both crates.

Solomon looked up from the crates of mortar bombs. He noticed the rear window of the Land Rover was rolled down. A mud-smeared man suddenly filled it. The man lobbed an object through the window.

Solomon turned and ran, shouting, "Kiins! Lift off! Lift off! Go! Go! Go!"

Kiins shoved his throttles forward and watched his team scatter.

The American had been hiding under the Land Rover. He ran five steps into the clearing and jumped on top of a shrub.

The shrub crumpled beneath him and he disappeared into the earth like Bugs Bunny jumping into his rabbit hole.

Time compressed.

The helicopter's skids lifted off the ground.

Flame shot out of the windows of the Land Rover. The body panels blew outward. The left fender revolved through the air and scythed through Solomon's spine like a meat cleaver. The members of the security team were burned and dismembered in the superheated blast wave as the remaining mortar bombs detonated.

The Land Rover's engine block flew through the cockpit of the helicopter like a flaming six hundred pound fist and blotted Kiins out of existence.

A few seconds passed and the final bits of flying Land Rover finally fell back to Earth.

Bolan crawled from his smoking hole. He yawned to alleviate the ringing in his ears. The nose of the helicopter was crumpled in like someone had hit it with a shovel. The rotor blades had dug a new trench inches from Bolan's bolt-hole. The fuselage was mostly intact, but it was beginning to burn in earnest. Bits of smoldering Land Rover littered the clearing.

Calvin James came out of the jungle and surveyed their handiwork. "Nice."

Bolan took the G-36 rifle he offered. Red came out of the trees and stepped as close to the burning chopper as he could. He shook his head as he gave its contents a quick examination. "Not too much salvageable. Guns, communications, its all a wash."

Denial had been Bolan's primary goal, and he had all the communication gear he needed at the moment. He clicked on his stolen com link. "Hey, buddy."

James and Red both put in their earpieces. This was going to be good.

21

The Triple Witch

"Hey, buddy."

Craig turned and glanced at the speaker monitoring the Russian tactical link. He raised an eyebrow. His opponent was ready to talk.

"Scratch helicopter number two," the American said.

Craig glanced at the woman. She was quietly and furiously trying to communicate with the helicopter. She shook her head and made a thumbs-down motion. The line was dead.

Craig kept his tone neutral. "Really."

"You have one hour to vacate the island. After that no prisoners will be taken and no quarter given."

The look on Craig's face made Smakofani consider jumping off *The Triple Witch* and swimming back to Hawaii.

"Very well." He spoke with the tone of ugly amusement. "No prisoners taken, no quarter given."

Craig punched a button on his desk and the line went dead.

BOLAN CLICKED OFF his transmitter.

Red shrugged in confusion. "So…what just happened?"

"Craig's insane." Bolan stared at the burning helicopter. "So I gambled."

Red raised a mangled eyebrow. "And?"

"I lost."

Red's shoulders sank. "You were bluffing?"

"No." Bolan turned away from the flames. "But neither is Craig."

"So what does that mean?"

James sighed. He read the situation all too clearly. "It means Craig has a Plan B."

"Plan B?" Red snorted. "He's out of helicopters, out of Land Rovers, out of gun jeeps, the Russians and the Pirates are down to half-strength. I know for a fact we've greased half his South Africans. What the hell kind of Plan B can he have?"

"Damned if I know," James conceded. "But you heard his voice. He has something. Some kind of option we don't know about, and we're about to feel it."

Red weighed everything he knew about Craig and what he had recently experienced at his hands. "Fuck."

THE SUBMARINE ROSE in the water like a dark behemoth. The Yuanzheng 23 was a Song-class diesel-electric and outdated by most modern standards. But diesel did have some advantages. One very specific benefit was being able to lurk very quietly.

The sub had been retrofitted with arriving undetected at unique and interesting locations in the Pacific Rim in mind.

Colonel King Kai gazed at *The Triple Witch*. He immediately wanted a yacht just like it. Colonel King was a senior member of the Communist Party in good standing. In public he was known for his savage discipline and dogmatic adherence to the principles laid forth by Chairman Mao. As a Special Forces operative, he had used his world travel and extensive connections to better himself in the black market.

He was known as a man who could get things done, brutal things, and he and his handpicked men did them quickly, quietly and with savage efficiency. These talents had brought him the favor of the Old Men in Beijing. His unique situation and capacities had also brought him the favor of the triads on the mainland, in Hong Kong and Taiwan. Between the rewards of service and his own personal activities Colonel King had amassed staggering and diversified holdings.

He expected Stephen Craig to add substantially to that personal fortune.

"Give me a firing solution on that vessel and flood torpedo tube Number Two," King ordered. "And keep the firing solution updated in case of movement."

Colonel King had dealt with the American billionaire before. It was best to have an ace up one's sleeve.

The Triple Witch lowered a dinghy while hatches on the hull of the Song-class sub opened and Special Forces troops began manhandling containers up onto the deck of the sub.

Craig watched from the bridge of *The Triple Witch*. His captain put a hand to his single earphone and nodded. "Mr. Craig, the sub has flooded a torpedo tube."

"Get me a firing solution on that son of a bitch," Craig replied.

The captain spoke quietly into the mike of his headset. In a concealed room in the central hull of *The Triple Witch*, a former United States naval weapons officer began punching coordinates into his weapons board.

The dinghy crossed to the submarine. Crates were loaded and the colonel and one of his men embarked.

Craig met Colonel King on the forward deck of the main hull. He smiled and held out his hand. "Kai, how are you?"

"It is good to see you again, Stephen. This is Sergeant Chien."

The sergeant nodded uncertainly at the American.

Craig gestured at the man with him. "This is Rutgers."

Colonel King knew of Rutgers. China's Military Intelligence kept a file on him and his group. He nodded.

Craig glanced at the crates being piled on his deck and smiled. "Is that what I think it is?"

King nodded at Chien. The sergeant levered open one of the crates with his combat knife. Inside were 120 mm rocket mortar bombs. The writing on the bombs was in Chinese characters, but each bomb had a series of color bands at the base of the warhead.

Rutgers recognized the code and turned on his heel in disgust.

"A mercenary with a sense of honor." King's eyes slitted like a hawk, boring holes in Rutgers's back as he walked away. "That is a dangerous combination."

"Rutgers is down to three men and no longer in command. I own his company. He doesn't get it back until this is over. Frankly, I've been keeping him around for tactical advice, however now that you are here his services are largely redundant," Craig said.

King accepted the wisdom of the statement and decided Rutgers and his surviving men would die tragically before the operation was over.

Craig stared at the submarine. "You have the tubes to hurl these bombs?"

"Yes, you explained the situation thoroughly. The mortars are in the hold, and will be transported to shore and assembled. These mortar bombs are rocket assisted. It would better if we had a helicopter laser designating the targets from the sky, but a topographical map will be enough for Sergeant Chien and his targeting computer."

Craig grinned. "Really."

"These bombs have an eight-mile range." The colonel nodded at the viability of the plan. "They can reach every village
on the island."

"THIS ISN'T GOOD." James handed Bolan the binoculars.

The Executioner stood on the promontory and eyed the
submarine. "What kind is it?"

"Dunno, hard to tell at this distance. She's kind of small,
and doesn't have any missile hatches up top. I'd make her a
hunter-killer, antishipping as opposed to a boomer carrying
nukes. Probably diesel-electric. If she is missile equipped,
they'll be cruise missiles, and she'll be slinging them out of
her torpedo tubes. "James shrugged. "Song-class, maybe.
I'm not totally up on the Chinese fleet."

Red grumbled unhappily. "So what in the blue hell are the
Chinese doing here? Much less cozying up with Craig?"

"Craig's cut a deal." Bolan watched the crates being unloaded and brought to shore. They were long and narrow. Others were obviously munitions canisters "Probably some kind
of profit-sharing scheme once mining resumes, the proceeds
being funneled through Hong Kong."

Bolan watched the figures in camouflage unloading cargo
up the narrow hatches in the hull. They were all wearing dis-
ruptive pattern jungle camouflage and carrying side arms.
"And those aren't sailors."

"Naw." Red spit in agreement. "Those are PRC special
purpose pricks if ever I've seen one. I don't know what's in
those crates—"

"Artillery of some kind. Without a helicopter and without
enough men to project force into the highlands Craig needs
something he can reach out and touch us with. These guys
and their cargo are the end game, Craig's ace in the hole, and
we are about to get hammered."

"So, uh…" Red ran a paw through his matted hair. "What do we do?"

"Red, I'm going to need those two 70 mm pack howitzers."

"The two pack—Jesus Christ!" Red threw his hands up in the air. "We both know what the hell they're unpacking! It's got to be goddamn mortars! Big ones! Big tubes! Twice our size and ten times our range! And you want to trundle those two little rusting pieces of shit down the mountain and trade artillery barrages?

"No."

"Striker, you are nuts!" Red waved his arms. "We'll be blasted apart in the first salvo!"

"I know that."

"You know that?"

"I know that."

Red turned to Calvin James. "He knows!" The massive ex-Marine whirled back on Bolan. "So just what the hell do you hope to accomplish?"

Bolan told him what he hoped to accomplish, and how.

"Calvin, get the drums beating. I need every man on this island still willing to fight assembled by dawn."

James laughed. "You know, Striker, you've come up with some wild stuff before, but this, this is…"

"Yeah, I know," Bolan said.

22

The rain poured straight down out of the night sky. Rutgers stood in the warehouse. Steam rose off him as the tin roof rattled. Not a single native remained in the township of the Church of England. The only Pa'ahnuians still in residence lay in the charred piles where their bodies had been burned. Their remaining bones and ash would be bulldozed into containers and sunk offshore.

Such would be the fate of the entire population of the island.

Rutgers examined the warehouse's new occupants. Crates of ammunition surrounded the half-dozen 120 mm mortars. A few crates were high explosives, but most were marked with chemical munitions warning codes.

They were Tabun gas bombs.

Tabun was nerve gas. The colorless, odorless nerve agent would extinguish the lives of the unprotected natives within seconds, with the added benefit of leaving no scars or bullet wounds.

The plan was simple

Craig and the mining company would declare that a contagion had swept the island. Health officials from the People's Republic of China would volunteer their assistance in controlling the contagion. With the island blockaded and safe from prying eyes, Craig and Colonel King would kill every last

Pa'ahnuian man, woman and child on the island. The villages would be burned. All the casualties on both sides of the conflict would be burned. All physical evidence of what had transpired on Pa'ahnui would be buried at the bottom of the Coral Sea Basin.

The island would be quarantined until the PRC health officials declared the mystery virus to have burned itself out.

Mining would resume on an island blissfully free of native habitation.

Bryce Delvoix pulled a cigarette out of his pack with his lips. "It's an abomination."

Delvoix was the dirtiest bastard Rutgers had ever met. But even he had his limits.

Rutgers snapped open his tarnished lighter and lit the cigarette. "Indeed, Bryce. It is."

Delvoix took a deep drag and eyed the mortars. "What do you figure the range is, then?"

"With rocket-assisted rounds? Six miles? Seven? Enough to reach any point on the island. They can go right over the top of the volcano." Rutgers glanced at the folding table with a map of the island on it. Red Xs with written coordinates marked every center of habitation on the island.

Delvoix exhaled blue smoke uneasily. "Genocide, then."

"Yes, Bryce. Genocide."

Gotwald slipped through the warehouse door and shook the rain from his poncho. "The jeep is ready, Commander. It's running, but barely. I don't know how far it will take us."

"All it has to do is get us into the jungle, Steppan. Then we'll hide it. Did you manage to get what I asked for?"

"Yes, Commander. The jeep is loaded with twenty of the extra AK-74s, each with a bandolier of spare magazines. I also liberated three cases of ammunition."

"Good." If they were going to join the revolution, they would sure as hell have to come bearing gifts to avoid winding up in the village soup pot. Rutgers returned his attention to the mortars. "And you, Bryce. Have you got what I asked you for, then?"

"Why yes, Commander." His pale blue eyes twinkled with uncharacteristic glee as he reached under his rain slicker and produced a seven-stick bundle of dynamite. "I happen to have it right here."

Rutgers nodded. "How long?"

"Fifteen seconds, Commander."

Rutgers idly wished there was enough time to wheel one of the mortars out and slam a few high-explosive rounds into *The Triple Witch* and the Chinese submarine, but they would be cut down before they could range. Destroying the mortars, the gas, and all the stored weapons, munitions and equipment in the warehouse would have to do for one night.

"Gotwald, go get in the jeep. We will be coming out directly." Rutgers snapped open his lighter again and held out the flickering flame. "You ready, Bryce?"

Delvoix held up the dynamite and presented the fuse.

Gotwald opened the door a crack and slipped out. He took one step and then came apart as a minigun burst walked up his body from his crotch to his skull. His body slumped to the floor as the last rounds ricocheted off the door frame.

Rutgers and Delvoix threw themselves down. Delvoix tucked the dynamite under his stump and drew his pistol. Rutgers unlocked the folding stock of the carbine he'd hidden under his poncho. The door banged wildly as the wind gusted and the rain poured inside the entrance.

Craig's voice crackled from the loudspeaker in the warehouse rafters. "Rutgers, what are you doing in there?"

Rutgers looked at Delvoix, who rolled his eyes.

"Why don't you come out and let's talk about this, while you still can?" Craig suggested.

Rutgers had seen the conversations Craig had engaged in with Hitihiti and the redheaded American. The prospects of surviving any "talk" with Craig were dismal at best.

"Bryce?"

Delvoix reclined against a pallet of mining equipment smoking. He took a long pull on his cigarette and savored the flavor. He holstered his pistol and took the dynamite out from under his stump. "You know. I had a feeling this would come to a bad end."

"I know."

"You're surrounded, Rutgers. Come out. Now."

Delvoix sucked on through his cigarette until it glowed fiery red. He brought the dynamite fuse inches from the tip. "I don't much fancy coming out of the ass end of that bastard's dogs," he said.

"Neither do I."

Delvoix raised an eyebrow and waited for his last order.

Rutgers nodded once. "Do it."

Delvoix tipped the fuse against his cigarette. The fuse suddenly sparked and hissed, and he tossed the bundle of dynamite among the crates of Chinese mortar bombs. He drew his pistol. "Nice knowing you, Commander."

"Last chance," Craig's voice announced.

Rutgers glanced around the warehouse. "You want to try the back door, for fun?"

Delvoix took a final drag on his cigarette. "We'll never make it."

The two mercs broke for the back door like Butch Cassidy and the Sundance Kid in their final moment.

The warehouse lit up like Doomsday.

THE BLAST ROLLED OVER the Land Rover like a wave. The corrugated walls of the warehouse blew out and flame engulfed the pirates surrounding it.

"A mercenary with a code of honor." Colonel King turned to Craig. "I told you it was a dangerous combination."

Craig could not stand hearing "I told you so." King did not know it, but he had just designated himself dog chow at the first convenient opportunity.

"Well," Craig said as he watched the remains of the warehouse as it burned to the foundations. "This is a setback."

King scowled into the flames. "I believe a response would be appropriate."

"Oh?" Craig perked up with interest.

King clicked on his personal com link and spoke in Mandarin.

Craig's voice was neutral. "What are you doing?"

King pointed toward the water behind them. "Watch."

Craig considered shooting King where he sat. They sat for five minutes.

A plume of rocket fire erupted out of the harbor water. Five seconds later a second rose up. Followed by a third, a fourth and fifth at five-second intervals. The missiles climbed into the sky at a shallow angle and the solid rocket boosters flamed out and fell away. The Land Rover vibrated again and again as five turbojet engines of the antiship missiles screamed into life and accelerated overhead.

"The rebels will be clustering in the highlands. When they see the fires here in the township, they may become emboldened. I thought it would be best to subject them to a preemptory missile bombardment," King stated.

Craig stopped just short of clapping his hands with childlike delight as the fifth missile streaked by overhead. Colonel King had just earned himself a temporary stay of execution.

BRYCE DELVOIX crawled.

He had become aware of the fact that he was still alive when he found himself near the edge of the town beneath the sheltering arc of a smoldering bulldozer blade. He did not remember crawling to it. He suspected he had been thrown there and the blade had fallen on top of him. He had been wearing his body armor and his helmet beneath his slicker, and they had probably saved his life. Most of his rain slicker had melted onto his body. He knew he was badly burned. His right eye was a throbbing pocket of cauterized tissue.

He crawled to the perimeter and then slid down the entrenchment. It had taken all of his strength to climb up the other side. He wearily belly crawled across the no-man's land. He hoped the rain and the burning warehouse would be distraction enough as he dragged himself toward the shelter of the tree line.

It wasn't.

"Hey!" Voices shouted behind him in Russian.

The trees were ten yards away.

He didn't make it.

A boot brutally lifted his chin and another shoved him onto his back. Delvoix fumbled for his pistol, but a boot to the side of his head sent stars exploding behind his remaining eye. The Russians stared down like invaders from Mars beneath their ponchos and night-vision goggles. The brutal sneers twisting their lips were very human.

The two Russians reached down to hoist Delvoix up. One of them staggered backward and fell as a submachine gun suddenly rattled from the trees. The second Russian stood and tried to bring his rifle to bear. A second burst caught him across the belly and a third snapped back his head and dropped him to the sand.

Delvoix lay unmoving in the rain.

He slowly became aware of a man and a dog standing over him. The man wore a sodden floppy hat and was armed with an archaic submachine gun. The dog sniffed at Delvoix suspiciously.

"G'day," the man said. "You rooted the shack?"

Delvoix considered this through the haze of his concussion. "Yes."

"Any of your mates about?"

"No. The rest are dead."

"Right, then." Inspector Filmoore stripped the dead Russians of their weapons and hauled Delvoix to his feet. The Australian draped the South African's remaining arm over his shoulder and turned back toward the jungle. "Welcome to the revolution," he said.

"WHAT IS THAT?" Sh'sho lifted his head.

Calvin James scanned the rain-blackened sky. "Fast movers."

Bolan listened to the roar of engines as they rapidly approached. They were too high-pitched to be jet fighters or transports. Bolan shot to his feet. "Sho! Evacuate the village!"

Sh'sho leaped to his feet shouting in his native tongue. The natives began scattering and grabbing their wives and children from the huts. People were running in all directions. They did not know what they were running from. They only knew its sound. The screams of the subsonic jet engines drowned out everything else as the cruise missiles adjusted their trajectories in their final seconds of flight.

The longhouse disappeared as it was struck at just under the speed of sound by 165 kilograms of high explosives. The second missile was five seconds behind. Missiles number three, four and five followed. The proximity of the buildings and their reed-and-wood construction left everything else in the village vulnerable to the multiple blast waves.

Bolan stood up from his cover in the trees.

Sh'sho stood at the edge of the clearing. He held his pistol in one hand and a samurai sword in the other, as he watched his village burn.

The survivors in the trees hunkered down weeping and shuddering as they heard the scream of the turbojets. They did not come. They faded into the distance and then lit up the horizon farther east of their village. Orange lightning strikes and rolls of thunder sounded in the distance.

The villages of the highlands were being systematically reduced.

Sh'sho turned to Bolan. "I told you earlier today I needed to speak with the elders. With the other village leaders. I told them your plan. Many did not wish to fight. They said it will be suicide."

Tears spilled down Sh'sho's dark face.

"All will follow you now."

23

"Red skies at night, sailor's delight…" Big Red stared out across the water.

"Red skies at morning, sailor take warning." Calvin James finished the saying.

Bolan took in the sun as it rose over the Pacific. It was red as blood. There was going to be a storm.

He turned back to the matters at hand and the war canoe the men of the village were preparing. It was a double outrigger of massive proportions. It would take at least twenty men to paddle it.

Sh'sho spoke quietly with the village headman. All of the men of the fishing village were present. Everyone who wasn't hauling carried a fishing spear, a machete or both. They were ready to fight. Sh'sho turned to Bolan. "Headman say each village on coast have one war canoe. Rest of the boats are regular size, for fishing, can hold four men."

There were seven coastal villages on Pa'ahnui.

"Tell him I need his war canoe. Tell him I need all of them. I need every canoe and fishing boat on this island, and every man willing to fight."

Sh'sho translated and the old man nodded. It was not news. Drums had been talking across the island all night, and the warriors of Pa'ahnui were gathering. Only twenty-five of

Red's trained men remained, but they stood with their ancient rifles ready and their bayonets fixed.

Bolan turned his attention to the artillery. "Can you do it, Red?"

Red looked at the ridiculous pair of cannons. Their barrels were only thirty inches long and with their pierced steel wheels they looked like small pieces of railroad equipment rather than artillery. He did not like the rusty barrels, the pitted bores and the sloppy tolerance of the firing pins.

"I been thinking about it, those war canoes are big, they probably won't capsize outright, but we're gonna have to bind the cannon down and when they fire the recoil force has to go someplace. I'm betting repeated firing will crack the hulls. Add the weight of twenty men paddling and any kind of surf conditions…" Red glanced warily at the ruby red skies. "And I figure these canoes will come apart like matchsticks with four or five shots."

"Okay." Bolan smiled dryly. "Now tell me what's really bothering you."

"Striker, I want to say this once, and for the record. The Japanese used double-based powder in their cannon shells."

"And?"

"That means they cut their gunpowder with nitroglycerine to give the propellant more oomph. And there's two things that ain't good for nitro—heat and age." Red cast a very wary eye on their pile of remaining cannon shells. "That ammo is more than half a century old and has been improperly stored in a tropical environment."

"Bottom line, Red."

"Bottom line is there is a very good chance that the nitro has sweated out of the powder mix and pooled in some or all of those shells."

"You're saying they're duds?"

"Duds? Oh hell no! I'm saying that when the hammer drops there's a real good chance that rather than getting a fast-burning propellant charge you're going to get a detonation. The cannons can't take that. When the pooled nitro detonates, so will the warhead. Then the barrel will burst and the breech-block will rip out of its collar and fly backward, violently, probably cutting half the rowers into shreds and smashing the canoe to kindling." Red raised a cautioning finger. "And that's not even considering what will happen to the ammo piled next to it."

"Any way you can check them?"

Red held up a shell casing he'd pried the warhead from. "Smell."

It smelled like gunpowder.

"Now try this one."

Bolan sniffed. The harsh, iodine-chemical smell of nitroglycerine was distinct. "That one pooled."

"That's right."

"You're saying you'll have to ruin each shell to be sure."

Red poured out the propellant and kicked sand over it. "Right."

Bolan shook his head. They just couldn't catch a break. "All right, do what you can without prying them open. Give each one a good sniff, see if you can tell anything. Try rotating them, tilt them up and down gently, see if the gunpowder shifts distinctly like sand or if it sounds clumpy."

"Well, shit, that's no goddamn guarantee of any—"

"Then find some paint or something, put a dot on the ones you're willing to bet on and toss the rest. We're only going to get off a few shots anyway. Meantime, get men to work on mounting them in the canoes."

"Someone's going to get killed."

Bolan nodded. "A lot of people are going to get killed, Red, and we have to have those cannons."

"But—"

"Explain the situation to the men, and then ask for volunteers."

Red grimaced. "This just bites."

There was a commotion near the edge of the village. People were cheering. Inspector Filmoore and his dog, Blue, came walking out of the bush. Walking next to them was what appeared to be a burned and abused side of beef. The meat was missing its left arm and right eye.

"G'day," the inspector said. "Nice to see you still with us, Striker."

"Inspector."

Filmoore handed a pair of AK-74 carbines and ammo to James. "This here is Bryce Delvoix. Last of the Executive Options lads. Ran into him outside the perimeter. Some Russian blokes were giving him a hard time of it." He nodded at Delvoix's condition. "There was an explosion in town last night."

Delvoix's pale blue eye peered out of a blistered, swollen and smoke blackened face. He measured Bolan. "You're the commando, then."

Bolan nodded. "One of them. Anything you can tell me about what happened in town?"

"The Chinese brought nerve gas and artillery mortars."

Bolan, James and Red stiffened.

Bryce shrugged. "We blew it up."

"Really."

The South African spit. "We may be mercenaries, but we're not Hitler."

"Rutgers is dead?"

"I think so, but then again, I made it. If he's not dead…" Delvoix sighed wearily. "He probably wishes he was."

Everyone assembled imagined their own fate at Craig's hands.

"Can you tell me anything about how many men and weapons Craig has, and their disposition?"

"Get me a piece of paper and a pen." Delvoix brightened. "I'll give you a complete inventory."

The Triple Witch

"So what is your plan?" Colonel King sipped beer. "I do not see how the operation can proceed without the nerve gas. You must realize my country's stockpiles are monitored very carefully by Military Intelligence. It will take time to get more."

"The plan remains unchanged," Craig replied.

"Please explain to me the exact plan."

Craig held up a bullet. "Total extermination of the native population."

"One native, one bullet at a time? That could take significant time and effort."

"I'm budgeting two weeks." Craig examined the remnants of the town out the window. "You brought a platoon of your men, and the sub has a crew of one hundred, roughly half of whom can be temporarily released from duty to assist us. I still have over one hundred Russians, pirates and personal troops. We have night-vision equipment. We start with the coastal villages. One by one, surfacing just offshore. We surround locals, round them up, tell them they are being relocated and then slaughter them. We still have one minigun. Line them up and each village should take about four seconds. We should have the entire coast depopulated in two days. Then we work our way inland to the valleys and finally the highlands. The bodies are burned and dumped at sea. The method of operation and cover story remain the same. Have your friends send in the medical teams as scheduled to corroborate the story."

King considered the genocide and found it did not bother him. "The submarine crew may balk at shooting women and children."

"Then they can pour the gasoline and roast marshmallows." Craig laughed. "But everyone participates in this. I don't want anyone with clean hands. Everyone has to have a stake in keeping things secret. Rumors we don't give a shit about, but I don't want anyone testifying before the world court."

"Perhaps it would be best then if the submarine sank and was lost with all hands upon departure," King suggested.

"Excellent idea. We start Operation Deinfestation at dawn." Craig smiled.

IT WAS RAINING AGAIN, but perhaps that was to their advantage. Night had fallen, and surprise was the only edge they would have. Bolan examined the fleet.

He had seven war canoes.

Two of the canoes had cannons mounted in the prows with rope. The third would carry their one remaining Japanese light machine gun. The rest would carry squads of riflemen. They also had a swarm of smaller canoes. These would be loaded with men armed with spears, machetes and war clubs. It had been an ugly choice, but Bolan had decided against the more modern fishing and motor boats. The enemy had a submarine. They would pick up the motor noise from miles away if they were listening, and their missiles could easily designate and destroy a fishing boat. The canoes were all made of wood and fabric, and with any luck the rain and surf would cover or disguise the sound of paddling in the ears of the passive sonar on the sub.

Bolan had quickly looked over his volunteers and picked four hundred to put under oars. Just about one hundred of them had firearms. However, they had other weapons. James had taken the land mines and explosives they had liberated from the first helicopter. They had twenty men armed with sixteen-foot bamboo pikes. Rather than stone spearheads, their weapons were tipped with Claymores, antitank and antipersonnel mines. The ordnance had been rigged with rip cords. The pikemen would ram their spears against their targets and yank the cord. The Japanese had used the same tactic against U.S. tanks during the war in the Pacific.

It had failed spectacularly.

They also had a small assortment of the remaining pipe bombs, mortar bombs, Molotov cocktails and a small pile of very suspicious 70 mm cannon shells.

James surveyed the armada. "This is going to be good."

Bolan turned his face into the rain. The wind was getting stronger and the surf turning to chop. "And whose jackass idea was it to come here?"

James refused to take the bait. "This is going to be good."

24

The Triple Witch

Craig ate lobster. Lizabet Smakofani sat beside him in a black cocktail dress. She looked radiant despite her arm being in a sling, and the bandages on her shoulder. Somehow the bloody bandaging on her bronze flesh made her ooze even more animal magnetism than usual. Gaz and Gabriello sat in the dining room eating lobster with the wrong fork and guzzling expensive champagne as if it were cheap beer. It was best that they were wearing bibs. They could not keep their eyes from crawling all over the woman. Even Colonel King's usual poker face slipped as he slid his eyes in her direction.

The woman ate lobster and drank champagne with the gusto of an impeccably mannered she-wolf.

Craig held up his glass and a crewman poured him more champagne. "Tell me, Kai, what do your scouts report?"

Colonel King had deployed a half-dozen, two-man teams at dusk. King sipped champagne. "The highlands seem almost entirely deserted. The missile bombardment drove them from the villages. Their grain storage and pig enclosures are destroyed. They have no food. Many of the coastal villages are deserted as well. One of my teams has detected a large encampment in the farthest river valley consisting mostly of women, children and the old. It appears the natives are abandoning the mountains and the coast and are concentrating in camps near the central river valleys where there is adequate water and some food." King smiled. "It should make the clean up much easier."

"What about their warriors?" Craig asked.

"They seem to have dispersed, probably into the jungle to regroup. My scouts report the drums have been active all night. I have a scouting team hunting one of the drummers as we speak. He will be brought back and tortured into translating for us. In the meantime, once we begin rounding up their women and children the warriors will come to us, either to fight, or most likely surrender. Either way extermination will be a simple matter after that. I have a container vessel coming with three helicopters—civilian models with medical markings. All are equipped with weapons stations and infrared imaging equipment. Pockets of holdouts or stragglers will be easy to detect. In the end, the rebels cannot get around the fact that this is a small island. Once we have achieved strategic control there will be no place to hide."

Colonel King's cell phone rang. "What is it?" King said into the phone.

"Colonel, passive sonar had detected some unusual background noise."

"What kind of noise?"

"It is dispersed and anomalous. The sonar operator cannot identify it. The computer does not recognize it as anything occurring in the sound catalog."

King frowned. "You have my permission to go active," he said.

King waited for the results. "Captain?"

"Indeterminate. The sound is near or on the surface. Rain and wind conditions are interfering."

It certainly couldn't be a ship. The sonar image of surface ships were not anomalous and dispersed, rain or no rain. King relayed the information to Craig.

Craig lost his smile as he rose from the table. "Fletcher, flares, now."

Captain Fletcher jerked his head at the first mate who ran from the room. Craig moved toward the bridge and the rest of the dinner party rose and followed him. The rainy night lit up as flare dispensers fired in a diamond pattern from the decks of *The Triple Witch*. The flares shot up into the black sky and suddenly blossomed into incandescent white light, illuminating the surrounding waters for hundreds of yards.

King shouted into his cell phone. "Gan!"

"What is it, Colonel?"

"Dive! Dive! Dive!"

Craig drew a Sig-Sauer P226 pistol from beneath his dinner jacket. "Captain Fletcher."

Fletcher stared in horror at the water. "Yes…Mr. Craig?"

"All hands, prepare to repel boarders."

Across the black water war canoes loaded with natives were bearing down on the two vessels.

"Fire!"

Big Red yanked the firing lanyard and the 70 mm howitzer boomed. The nose of the war canoe rose with the recoil and the ropes and planks holding the cannon in place squealed and shifted. The night was pitch-black and the rain sleeted into their faces, but the massive trimaran was lit up like the Disneyland Parade of Lights.

The shell hit the ship broadside and blasted a hole in her starboard hull.

Five hundred natives roared savagely.

"Reload!"

Bolan had hoped to get a lot closer before opening fire, but the flares had settled that. They would be sitting ducks to anyone on deck with a rifle. Bolan stood in the middle of the canoe and roared at the men in the back. "Drums! Now!"

They had to cover the intervening two hundred yards. They needed speed.

Calvin James's canoe blossomed into orange fire and the black sail of the sub took a direct hit.

The drummers began pounding at full racing rhythm. The rowers dipped their paddles and stroked relentlessly with every thud. Every man not engaged in paddling began firing their rifles and pistols at the two moored vessels.

Red yanked the open breech and ejected the smoking brass shell. Matt Ka'Kaio handed him a fresh round, and he rammed it home and slammed the breech. There was no way to aim save by pointing the canoe. The prow was pointed like an arrow straight at *The Triple Witch*.

"Fire!"

The cannon belched orange fire and the entire canoe shuddered as the ancient wood took the recoil energy. The canoe's prow rose up and the paddlers dug into the waves to regain lost momentum. The clamshell door on the starboard hull of *The Triple Witch* blasted inward and buckled.

"Reload!"

Dark-suited men were boiling onto the deck of the trimaran. Rifles began cracking and popping in their hands as they returned fire.

The water around the submarine began roiling as it took on ballast to dive. James's cannon boomed a second time, and the sub took a hit to the hull right on the waterline.

They closed to one hundred yards.

Bolan raised his G-36 rifle and began firing short bursts at the men on the decks of *The Triple Witch*. Red fired the cannon, and the third round smashed into the starboard hull of the trimaran. With two holes in the hull at the waterline and the clamshell doors buckled the starboard hull was rapidly taking on water. *The Triple Witch* was tipping slightly but it would take a lot more to sink her.

"Shit!" Red pulled the firing lanyard and nothing happened. He heaved open the breech and yanked out the dud.

The canoes skimmed up upon the sub.

Bolan shouted above the sound of the wind and the guns. "Pikes! One! Two! Three! Four!"

Sh'sho bellowed out a translation, but it was not needed. Each native knew his assignment. Four men with antitank mines mounted on the end of the their pikes rammed the sixteen-foot bamboo poles against the black behemoth of the sub. They rammed them down beneath the waterline and yanked the rip cords as they made contact.

Orange light flashed beneath the waves. The shaped-charge warheads were designed to burn a hole in tank armor and send a jet of superheated molten metal and gas within to kill the crew. The jets burned through the rubber acoustic tiles and outer skin of the sub and blasted through the pressure hull. Superheated fire and gas shot into the compartments within.

Calvin James leaped out of his canoe and onto the deck of the sub. The deck was already under a foot of water and receding. One of the pikemen followed him. James ran to the sail as it began to slide beneath the water like a giant shark fin. The hole in the sail belched black smoke. James climbed onto the sail and his pikeman jumped up with him.

"Now!"

The pikeman rammed his charge against the hatch cover. The hatch buckled and burned beneath the superheated fury of the shaped charge.

They jumped back as gunfire erupted from the ruptured hatch.

James unslung his satchel charge. It was really more of a canvas bag containing three of the remaining mortar bombs with a pipe bomb for a fuse. He lit the fuse and threw it down the hatch. His canoe had already continued onward toward *The Triple Witch*.

James and his assistant dived into the water and swam to the next target.

"MULTIPLE BREACHES in the pressure hull!" The first mate had lost his composure and was nearly screaming in panic. Red lights were blinking throughout the attack center of the sub. Only a skeletal crew was on board. The rest had been issued weapons from the armory and were assisting with preparations in town for the terminal phase of the island clearing operation.

"Take on ballast! Dive! Dive! Dive!"

Captain Gan whirled as orange fire lit up the hatchway behind him. Heat washed across his face and the men in the next compartment screamed as they were sprayed with molten metal and superheated gas. Water began pouring into the breach in the superstructure and turned into steam.

"Seal that hatch!"

Three more detonations rapidly shook the hull.

"Captain! Flooding in compartments, five, seven and nine! There is a major breach in compartment eight and the sail."

The sub shuddered as the molten metal of one of the shaped charges burned into the oxygen-rich mixture of the starboard air tank and ignited it. Fire ripped through the cabins on the starboard side.

"Batten all hatches!"

"Captain! We are flooding!"

"Just take us down five meters where they can't reach us! Then load—"

Another blast of heat washed over Captain Gan. This one came right down the gangway from the sail and singed his face. Gan drew his pistol and began firing back up through the breached hatch.

Captain Gan listened to his crew screaming on all decks and his own panic mounted. The submarine had broken open. She was dying. If they submerged, they would never surface again. He snarled at the helmsman. "Blow ballast! All engines full speed ahead! Emergency war power! Helmsman! The beach! Run us aground!"

A bulky sack banged and clanked down the ladder and fell at Captain Gan's feet. It was sparking and fusing.

Gan's face went white with horror.

The fireball filled the command center. The blast wave ruptured the hatches between it and the next deck and rolled in a wave through the bulkheads that had not been closed yet.

The helmsman had been incinerated in his chair before he could blow ballast and reverse the submarine's descent. The sub continued to dive, taking on ballast and continuing to take in water through the wide-open ruptures in the hull and sail. The air tanks were bursting into flames and the parts of the sub that were not flooding were on fire. The sub's descent trajectory ceased any semblance of a dive. She was sinking like a stone. This close to shore the sea bottom was only a hundred yards below the surface.

She had not quite reached the sea floor when the fires reached her missile bays.

The Triple Witch

CAPTAIN FLETCHER STOOD on the bridge. He watched as orange fire erupted from the Chinese sub. He checked the loads in his rifle. The war canoes came on with every beat of the drums.

Stephen Craig was shrugging into his body armor. "I make it several hundred at least."

Fletcher clicked his bayonet onto the end of his rifle. There were several hundred blood-crazed islanders in war canoes paddling furiously toward his ship. They had just sunk the submarine, and the Chinese Special Forces troops, the Russian mercenaries and the Filipino pirates were all on shore getting their beauty sleep in preparation for the morning's slaughter.

Gabriello stared at the oncoming outriggers disbelievingly. He was a pirate. The natives of the islands he raided always ran for the trees.

Now they were coming for him.

Gaz looked close to panic. He knew what was in store for him if they took him alive.

Colonel King watched, stone-faced, as his submarine sank burning beneath the waves. Phone and radio communications with the sub had gone dead.

Captain Fletcher spoke into the intercom. "Weapons ready, Mr. Siders?"

The first mate spoke rapidly across the line. "Yes, Captain."

Fletcher looked at Craig. The billionaire seemed absolutely unperturbed as he clicked a magazine into his FN P-90 and checked the optical sight. He nodded at Fletcher.

Captain Fletcher punched his intercom button. "Fire at will."

The sound of the miniguns ripping into life was extremely comforting.

Gaz watched the carnage begin out the window.

"Ilya?"

Gaz turned back to Craig. "Yes, boss?"

Craig stared at the Russian with preternatural intensity. "I'm blaming this one on you."

Gaz' froze as he felt the muzzle of a machine pistol press into the back of his skull.

RED PULLED THE FIRING lanyard. The cannon did not fire. Instead there was a strange pop and a hiss. Red paled. "Shit!"

Bolan moved. "Red! Get—"

Burdick rammed his shoulder into Bolan and knocked him overboard. The Pacific closed over the soldier's head and a split second later the prow of the war canoe disappeared as the pooled nitroglycerine within the cannon shell detonated. Men spilled screaming in all directions as the canoe came apart and bits of metal ripped through the crew. The breech-block blasted out of its collar and ripped the rowers in two as it hurtled backward, trailing smoke and flame into the drummers. The canoe slammed back down into the water and cracked in two on its broken spine.

Bolan swallowed seawater and lost his G-36 as he kicked for the surface.

Red was gone.

Armageddon greeted him as he surfaced, and its harbinger was a howling snarl of miniguns firing at maximum rpm. Bolan dived and kicked beneath the waves. The wavering surface above flashed and strobed with the blast of orange fire, yellow muzzle-flashes and the flickering incandescent light of the descending flares. Bullets hissed through the water trailing streamers of bubbles.

Bolan kicked on beneath the waves, swimming until his vision began to darken. He reached out and his hand touched the smooth hull of *The Triple Witch*. Bolan rose to take a breath, then made his way to the prow and slipped between the buckled clamshell doors. His hands touched a steel ramp and he pressed himself up until his eyes broke the water.

A pair of crewmen with wrenches were desperately heaving on the hydraulic pistons.

Bolan rose out of the water. The two crewmen regarded him in slack-jawed horror. The soldier nodded. "Swim for shore."

The larger of the two crewmen screamed and came at Bolan swinging his four-foot steel wrench like a baseball bat. Bolan released his sword from its sheath and creased through the mechanic's throat in one gleaming motion. The man's momentum kept him moving forward until he fell face first into the dark water flooding the compartment. He bobbed motionless above the hydraulic ramp in a spreading cloud of scarlet.

The other man dropped his wrench and gave Bolan a sickly smile of surrender. Bolan jerked his head at the buckled door. "Swim."

The crewman hurled himself into the water and flailed his way out. Bolan entered the ship. At the back of his mind he acknowledged Burdick's death, but he'd have to mourn his friend later. He could hear the miniguns snarling above. They would reduce the islanders' attack to a slaughter in moments. The soldier sheathed his sword and clambered up the hydraulic cylinders inside the buckled door and pulled himself outside. Guns were firing in all directions. At least one-third of the canoes were now empty, and the water was littered with blasted bodies. Bolan could see fins cutting between the waves as sharks began savaging the dead and wounded. The remaining canoes were closing on *The Triple Witch,* but the miniguns were sweeping them like fire hoses. One of them seemed to be firing directly over Bolan's head. The Executioner got a foot on top of the door and levered himself up within range of the prow. He tottered precariously a moment on the buckled door frame and leapt for the rail.

Bolan's sword cleared its sheath as he heaved himself onto the deck.

Five feet away the two-man, minigun crew gaped in shock as the Executioner materialized beside them. The loader dropped his ammo pack and clawed for his pistol. The gunner began to swing his six barrels around as Bolan lunged and cut.

The gunner's hands fell from the grips of his minigun as Bolan cleaved off both his arms below the elbow. The gunner screamed and fell to the deck. Bolan's blade blurred. The loader was dead.

Bolan sheathed his bloodstained sword and leapt into the gun emplacement. He took the minigun's grips and swung the weapon around on its mount. He had a clear line on the aft gun position. He put the ring sight on the gun team and squeezed his trigger. The six barrels blurred into motion and tracers streaked from stem to stern. They impacted the aft gun position in a shower of sparks and blood. Bolan swept the position of the riflemen on the upper decks that had been firing into the native flotilla. The minigun fell silent as Bolan ran out of living targets. He swung his six muzzles on the central hull of the trimaran.

Stephen Craig was watching the proceedings impassively from the swept window of the bridge.

Bolan squeezed his trigger and held it down.

Seven hundred rounds burned into the bridge before the minigun whirled on an empty chamber. Bolan released the trigger and the barrels clicked to a halt. Craig was gone. The Six-Pack's light bullets had failed to penetrate the armored glass of the bridge. Bolan took the loader's rifle and checked the loads.

Native canoes were thumping against the hull of *The Triple Witch*. The natives began swarming up over the side like ants.

The deck vibrated beneath his feet as the engines of *The Triple Witch* rumbled into life. If they started moving forward at any speed, they could beach themselves and the troops on shore would counterswarm the ship and finish the revolution once and for all. Bolan ran aft. He stabbed his fingers at two natives who still retained their pikes. "You!" Bolan waved them on and kept running.

A hardman popped up from a hatch in the deck and Bolan hammered his head apart with a burst from his rifle. Bolan skidded to a stop at the stern. The twin screws were beginning to churn up froth and the ship began to inch forward toward shore. Bolan pointed down at the maelstrom of the motor wash. The natives did not need any translation. They rammed their mine-tipped lances beneath the churning water and yanked their lanyards. The black water went orange and erupted into geysers of steam. The natives tossed away their shattered poles and took up their war clubs as the engines beneath them howled and groaned unnaturally. The ship's forward momentum slowed and stalled as oil began to bleed onto the waters like blood.

The Triple Witch was adrift.

The two natives followed Bolan as he ran across a gangway onto the central hull. The Pa'ahnuians had taken horrific casualties, but about half of them had reached the ship and the fight was going hand to hand as the natives came to grips with their enemy.

Bolan and his two men came to a door and the native war clubs easily splintered the teak panels. The soldier put a burst through the entryway as the door failed. They spilled into a luxuriously appointed guest cabin. Bolan heard feet thudding in the interior passageway as he kicked the door inward.

Edgar Gabriello was charging down the corridor with two of his men. Bolan fired on full-auto, and blood sprayed the walls of the passageway as the two leading pirates took the bursts point-blank. The rifle racked open on a smoking empty chamber. One of the Bolan's men charged past screaming a war cry. Gabriello shot him four times with a .357 Magnum Colt Python. Bolan lunged, throwing his empty rifle like a lumberjack at an ax throwing competition. The G-36 had time to revolve once before the barrel struck the pirate solidly in the face. Gabriello staggered back a step and the revolver fell from his hand. The second native lunged forward swinging his club.

Gabriello blinked into awareness behind his thick glasses. Steel instantly filled his hands from the sheaths in his sash. The Pa'ahnuian gasped and dropped his club as Gabriello's knife laid open his forearm to the bone. The pirate's *parang* slit open his face from his jaw to his eye. The native jerked his head back instinctively and bared his throat as Gabriello had intended.

The Pa'ahnuian sagged as his throat fell open from earlobe to earlobe. The three blade strokes had taken less than two heartbeats.

The native warrior was dead as he hit the floor.

Blood dripped down Gabriello's split brow and stained his teeth as he smiled at Bolan. He held his curving, scarlet-stained blades loosely in each hand.

Bolan drew his sword and took a low guard.

Gabriello smiled. He had trained in his native Filipino blade arts since early adolescence. They both knew Bolan was no samurai, and there was very little room to swing the twenty-eight-inch blade in the ship's corridor.

Bolan lunged. Gabriello deftly deflected the blow with his *parang* and Bolan felt the icy burn of the knife as it opened muscle above his elbow. Bolan leapt back. Only his own battle-honed reflexes saved him from having his fingers cut off as Gabriello sliced at his hand. Bolan's blade rang in his hands as steel met steel instead.

The pirate was snake-strike fast.

Bolan stumbled on a corpse and the pirate's foot whipped up and smashed Bolan in the chin. The soldier tasted blood as he tottered back. He kept his blade before him, using its length to keep Gabriello at bay as he shook his head desperately to clear it. The pirate stalked forward unconcernedly, grinning again as Bolan nearly tripped among the corpses littering the corridor. Gabriello's orangutan smile was painted on his face. He eyed the open flesh on Bolan's arm and the blood trickling down his chin.

Bolan raised his sword. He could already feel his left arm weakening.

Gabriello came in for the kill.

Bolan spit a mouthful of blood into Gabriello's face. Blood and spittle spattered across the lenses of his eyeglasses. Gabriello instinctively crossed his blades before him to stop his adversary's thrust.

The Executioner sliced instead.

Gabriello wheezed and dropped his blades as Bolan yanked the samurai sword free. The pirate fell dead to the carpet.

Bolan tore away Gabriello's sash and bound his elbow. He scooped up the fallen Colt Python revolver and checked the loads. Two rounds remained. He rose and continued down the corridor.

25

The Triple Witch

Calvin James dropped from the deck above and landed, cat-like, among the gunmen. A hardman turned into him and James plunged his combat knife up under the guard's armored vest and ripped him open from hipbone to hipbone. The man wheezed and folded forward. James yanked the G-36 rifle from his dying hands. The second gunman barely had time to look over his shoulder in surprise as James sprayed a burst through his spine.

Bryce Delvoix and a half-dozen natives moved forward. James ran his eye over the massive trimaran. Most of the fighting had ceased. Those guards who hadn't been overwhelmed had retreated inside. The tide had turned. It was no longer a siege. It was now a house-clearing operation. Filmoore and some of the natives with rifles were exchanging fire with some men up on top of the bridge.

Their losses had been horrific. Their armada had started out with over five hundred men and James doubted there were 150 effectives left. The water below was full of dead men and broken canoes. The decks were littered with bodies.

Sh'sho stripped the dead security men of their magazines and passed them around. "Where's Striker?"

"Dunno." James passed the two handguns to the natives and looked back toward the beach. The sea battle had attracted attention. Church of England was lit up, and armed men were running to the beach. "Bryce, take two men and get the inspector. I want the two of you on the miniguns facing the town. Lay suppressive fire down on the beach. We can't handle being counterboarded."

"Right." Delvoix tapped two natives and they followed him toward the prow of the ship.

"I think Striker's already gone after Craig. Sho, you and me have to storm the bridge and finish taking this tub." James put his foot onto the door and smashed it back off its hinges. He looked back at the natives. "But first, see if anyone has any mortar bombs left."

"Hey, lover."

Bolan spun, extending the .357 before him down the corridor. The woman slid from a stateroom down the corridor behind him. A 3-round burst from her .22-caliber machine pistol tracked the wall by Bolan's head. She staggered back as a .357 hollowpoint hammered her above the heart. Her face went ashen and the pistol fell from her hand. Bolan's second shot smashed her off her feet. He stalked forward with the spent revolver smoking in his hands. He kept it trained on the woman. She didn't know it was empty.

She groaned and looked up from the floor painfully as Bolan approached. She was wearing an armored vest over her cocktail dress and her armor had held. She looked up at Bolan and smiled.

"Get him! Get him! Get him!" she shouted.

The four Neapolitan mastiffs leapt from the stateroom.

Bolan flung his pistol at the lead dog and ran. The woman's laughter rang like a bell behind him. The soldier barreled down the corridor. He threw his shoulder into the door at the end of the hall. The lock snapped and the door flung open. Bolan slammed it shut behind him and scrabbled for the security chain. He chained the door just as the dogs hit it. Bolan was thrown back as six hundred pounds of war hound hit the lightweight interior door. The dogs made almost no noise, except for their ragged breathing and the slavering of their jaws as they tried to shove their heads through the narrow opening the chain allowed.

"Welcome."

Bolan whirled. His sword flashing in his hand.

Stephen Craig stood at the other end of the room, pointing the muzzle of his P-90 at Bolan.

Between the two men lay an abomination. Bolan had seen horrific atrocities firsthand and been exposed to the worst that humanity had to offer. What he saw before him was an example of how Craig dealt with failure.

Ilya Gaz had been tortured to death.

Bolan held his sword and considered the throw. There was hardly a worse missile weapon than a sword. Craig could burn all fifty rounds in his magazine into him before Bolan could even finish his windup.

Bolan had only one option, and that was to try to rattle Craig's cage. The Executioner knew something about battlefield psychology, and he had run into his fair share of sociopaths. They had movies going on in their heads, of how they saw themselves and how they wanted things to be. Through sheer force of will and ruthless effort Craig had built the wealth and the power to turn the movies in his head into live action, with the entire world a stage for enacting his twisted script. Like most sociopaths, his insanity was all about dominance and control. Messing with Craig's movie would probably turn him from a calculating sociopath into a violent psychotic. Bolan was wounded and exhausted. Craig was fresh, wearing body armor and his girlfriend was extremely dangerous, but going head to head with the psychopath was Bolan's only chance.

"I own your island. I own your boat. I own you." Bolan said as he slowly reversed his sword and spiked it into the floor. He mockingly beckoned Craig to come forward. "And I got something real for you in these hands."

Craig's smile returned to his face. His eyes seemed glazed in incomprehension or malfunction.

Bolan lunged.

He expected to feel the buzz saw bullet strikes of the P-90 cutting him apart. Instead he saw stars as Craig shot-putted the five-and-a-half-pound weapon into his face. Bolan raised his hands in a blind block and he felt the burning kiss of steel as Craig's knife cut a long line up the inside of his right arm and crossed his palm. Blood flew.

"Do tell," Craig said. He was still a lunatic, but his eyes were lucid once more.

Bolan stood his ground. Blood dripped across his face and lips from his cut forehead. He wondered if the main veins in his wrist had been severed, but he could not afford to look. His right hand could still make a fist, and that would have to be enough. He waited for Craig to close the distance and come in again with the knife.

The mastiffs slavered and lunged against the door. Their severed vocal cords turned their attempts to bark into grotesque, shuddering groans and hisses.

"Oh, I'm sorry." Craig held up his skinning knife. "Is this bothering you?"

Craig flung the knife point-first into the floor. He returned Bolan's gesture, beckoning him forward with both hands. "You were saying something?"

Bolan's left hand snaked forward, his spread fingers thrusting for Craig's eyes. Craig snapped his head aside but not quickly enough to save both eyes. Bolan's middle and forefinger sank into the man's right eye. Bolan's right hand came around in a savage roundhouse. The bloody cup of his right palm slammed across his adversary's ear. Craig's eardrum shattered and blood shot from his left nostril. Bolan's left elbow ripped upward. He intended to shatter Craig's jaw, but his elbow slid on the blood covering the man's chin. The bone of Bolan's elbow joint wiped Craig's nose up into his eyebrow, snapping his septum and cracking the nasal bone.

The three blows landed in just under a second. The collective shock and damage should have left Craig rolling on the floor screaming, if not prone, unconscious, and sliding into shock.

Instead, Craig's left hand closed around Bolan's throat like a vise. His right fist pistoned twice into Bolan's jaw. The billionaire flung Bolan to the floor, then walked across the room as if the extent of his injuries were little more than a bloody nose.

Craig yanked the sword out of the floor.

Bolan levered himself to his feet. He gazed at the fallen P-90 off to his right. Craig's single eye noted the look and grinned.

Bolan couldn't get to the gun without going through Craig, and that was suicide.

Craig came on, the ruins of his face hanging from his skull.

Bolan stiffened his middle and forefinger and drove them spearlike at Craig's remaining eye. His opponent caught the fingers and made a fist. Bolan snarled as his fingers fractured. Craig released the broken digits and seized the soldier by the throat with both hands. His fingers sank into Bolan's carotid arteries and trachea with sickening strength. Bolan deliberately dropped to his knees as his vision darkened. Even with his insane power Craig could not hold him up at arm's length.

Bolan rammed his forearm between Craig's legs.

The billionaire grunted as his testicles crushed. His grip loosened momentarily but did not release and he clawed Bolan's throat for renewed purchase. Pain would not stop Craig. Mortal injuries would not stop him.

The only way to stop Craig was to kill him.

Bolan rammed his broken hand into his adversary's throat. He seized him by the crotch with his other hand and stood. Craig's fingers shifted and tore into the flesh of Bolan's throat but remained in a death grip. The soldier groaned with effort as he pressed his burden over his head and lumbered forward toward the door. He used the last remains of his strength and both of their body weights to hurl Craig through the door.

Craig's grip tore loose from Bolan's neck and he crashed through the teak panels and fell amid the startled mastiffs. The Executioner fell to his knees, his vision doubling.

He had to get to the gun.

Craig rose like an unstoppable juggernaut.

He lashed out at the dogs. They were snarling and growling with rage. They smelled blood and sensed the damage on their master. He tried to command them, but he could do little more than stutter and drool past his broken jaw.

Craig kicked at one of the animals and fell.

For the first time in a lifetime ruled by fear and pain the pack sensed that the Alpha male was weak. The smell of his blood filled their nostrils. They were dogs that had been trained to kill and eat humans. The dogs attacked.

Craig's Kevlar body armor protected his torso. The dogs savaged everything that protruded out of it.

Bolan crawled for the P-90. It seemed to be miles away across the bloody floor.

Out in the corridor the woman screamed. Her machine pistol chattered and one of the dogs jerked, jumping, whirling, snapping behind it as it took a 3-round burst of .22-caliber bullets in the flank.

The dogs charged after the new prey.

The machine pistol fired twice more, and then the woman screamed.

She screamed again and again and then she was silent.

Bolan rose with the P-90 in his hands. He staggered toward the doorway. The corridor was a blood-drenched house of horror.

Bolan flicked the selector switch of the P-90 to full-auto and put the twisted beasts down easily.

He walked down the hall, stopped over the dead woman and shook his head.

The Executioner looked up at the sound of gunfire coming from the deck above. He went to Craig's corpse and took his spare magazines and liberated the contents of his shredded pockets. He retrieved his sword and walked back down the hall to rejoin the fight.

The Triple Witch still remained to be taken.

26

"They're all over the ship!" The first mate's fear betrayed him as his voice rose. Captain Fletcher stared unflinchingly, scowling as bullets smashed the bulletproof window on his bridge. The hundreds of available troops on shore were being prevented from coming to his aid by suppressive fire from his own miniguns. The first mate was right. The natives were all over the ship and breaching the interior compartments. The ship was dead in the water, and he didn't have enough sailors or security men left to counterattack. Craig and the woman were somewhere belowdecks playing sick games with Gaz.

The natives seemed to be everywhere at once, and Fletcher suspected a second wave would be coming any minute.

The pounding of the drums throbbed, and the natives screamed their war chants. Fletcher had one spare magazine for his Browning Hi-Power pistol. He glanced out the armored window at the waving machetes and spears and didn't much fancy being taken alive.

He went to the glass case mounted behind the tiller. He put the butt of his pistol through the glass and drew his British naval officer's sword. He put the gold hilted saber in his right hand and the pistol in his left. He hadn't carried the blade since his graduation parade from the British Naval Academy, but he felt significantly less vulnerable with the thirty-two and half inches of Solingen steel in his fist. "First mate! Put out a distress signal to the Papuan naval blockade! We are under naval siege by rebels and require immediate assistance."

Fletcher relaxed slightly as the first mate began chattering into his headset. King spoke a few words to his two bodyguards in Mandarin. Between the Chinese, Fletcher's crewmen and Craig's security team, there were ten armed men on the bridge. The window was armored glass and the door was security steel with key code access, and two more steel doors down the corridor further separated their redoubt from the enemy. Without power tools or welding torches it would take the natives hours to break in. Without their cannons they stood no chance at all of sinking the trimaran. Let them dance and shriek on the decks. A pair of navy patrol boats would end the siege nicely. Even if they were patrolling on the opposite end of the island they would be able to arrive within half an hour at most.

The first mate sighed with relief. "Captain, Papuan navy is sending two patrol boats, ETA fifteen minutes."

A spear bounced off the bridge window.

Fletcher had to give credit where credit was due. It had been one hell of an attempt. They had boarded his ship, but the rebellion was over. Fletcher turned to King. The colonel and his two bodyguards muttered to one another in Mandarin with their assault rifles at the ready.

"Colonel King, contact your men on shore and have them ready to deploy. The naval blockade ships have 40 mm cannons. I will instruct them to destroy the minigun positions on *The Triple Witch*. With the *Witch*'s guns silenced she will be open for your special purpose troops to counterboard. I will have the Papuans ferry your assault teams to *The Triple Witch*. Do you concur?"

"Indeed." King nodded. "I will have my men ready to—"

Fletcher followed King's distracted look out the window.

A half-naked black man was running across the flying deck straight at the bridge. In the red light of the flares, Fletcher could see he was an African rather than a Melanesian native. He did not have a rifle or spear or machete. His left hand stretched forward as he ran and his right was cocked back in a javelin-thrower's position. He held a cylindrical object in his right hand.

Fletcher's insides turned to ice water as his eyes focused on the conical brass tip of the object's impact detonator fuse. The man could clearly see Fletcher. He waggled his eyebrows and threw the bomb straight at him. The Japanese 50 mm mortar bomb flew in a beautiful spiral.

The grinning bomber threw himself over the rail.

"Bloody hell!" Fletcher shouted. "Down!"

The bridge window went orange with the detonation and blew inward in a lethal swarm of armored glass shards. Fletcher's ears rang and his vision pulsed, but he rose and began firing his pistol out the breached window as fast as he could pull the trigger. He could dimly hear the muted reports of the Chinese and Craig's guards spraying with their rifles.

A few of the surviving recessed red emergency lights clicked on. King's bodyguards had been knocked unconscious in the blast along with the first mate and one of Craig's hardmen. The gunfire inside and out suddenly ceased. Fletcher reloaded his pistol as he and Colonel King exchanged surprised looks. The natives hadn't swarmed.

A native's voice shouted from just out of sight. "Surrender! Now!"

Fletcher shouted back. "Papuan attack boats from the blockade will be here in ten minutes. They will sweep the decks with automatic cannons and then ferry Chinese Special Forces teams on board. I have ten men with automatic weapons in here. We'll slaughter anyone you send through that window. Lay down your arms and surrender!"

"Ten minutes?" There was a moment of silence while that was considered. "I have hundred men here. If we storm that bridge and more men die, you will suffer if you are taken alive."

Fletcher listened for a moment to the throb of the drums. He shook his head and looked at King. "Colonel, I suggest we surrender."

The muzzle of King's assault weapon pointed at Fletcher's head. "I do not surrender. Neither do you."

"One minute! Decide!" the voice shouted.

Fletcher raised an eyebrow. "How many spare magazines do you have?"

"I have these." King bent over one of his dead men and pulled a pair of beer can shaped cylinders out of his web gear.

"What are those?"

"Nerve gas grenades. Here is what I want you to do. Kill the deck lights on the outside of the ship. When the natives charge, I will throw the grenades out the window. The gas is colorless. They will undoubtedly be screaming when they charge. They will not see or hear the gas deploy. We will close the door behind us and hole up in the corridor. I suspect half or more will be dead before they know what is happening. The natives will panic. Even if they don't, we only need to hold them off until the Papuan navy arrives."

The idea of nerve gas made Fletcher sick. So did the idea of roasting rotisserie style over a native fire pit. "All right."

"Wait for the charge to start. Then kill the lights."

Fletcher nodded and raised his voice. "You come try it!"

"Not a good decision!" the voice shouted back. "Pa'ah-nui!"

One hundred natives roared in unison. "Pa'ahnui!"

King rose with his thumbs in the pins.

The steel door to the bridge opened with a soft pneumatic hiss.

Colonel King whirled with a grenade in each hand.

A figure filled the doorway. Flame spit from an automatic weapon. King staggered as he took hit after hit. He was wearing soft body armor, but that was exactly the type of protection the P-90's needlelike bullet was designed to defeat. King fell gurgling with twenty-five rounds through his chest. His arms flopped outward to either side like a cross.

His thumbs were still twined through the safety pins.

The natives were storming across the deck.

The Executioner and Captain Fletcher locked gazes. Bolan cocked his head at the sound of the charging Pa'ahnuians. "Craig's dead."

Fletcher eyed the gore-caked sword in Bolan's hand. "I don't doubt it."

"So are the woman, Gaz and Gabriello. I suggest you surrender."

Fletcher let out a long breath and then dropped his pistol. He presented his sword, hilt first, to Bolan. "The ship is yours."

"Everyone drop to your knees, hands behind your heads."

Fletcher and the remaining men on the bridge dropped. Bullets from the charging natives streaked through the window over their heads. Bolan knelt but held up the ancient Japanese sword so that the attacking mob could see the blade.

"Cease-fire!" James shouted. "Cease-fire"

The gunfire ceased, but everyone on the bridge could hear the panting of over a hundred men just outside the shattered window. Calvin James spoke quietly. His voice came from the roof right over the window. "Striker?"

"I have the bridge, Calvin."

James dropped down in front of the window. He held a hissing and sparking pipe bomb in one hand and his combat knife in the other. He pinched off the fuse of the pipe bomb. "Where's Red?"

"He was right about those cannon shells." Bolan shook his head. "He didn't make it."

James grimaced, then gestured to the crouching army on the deck. The natives rose.

Bolan gauged their mood. "Sho?"

Sh'sho was in the front rank, a samurai sword and a Russian machine pistol filling his hands. Both were covered with blood. "Yes, Striker."

"I have accepted the captain's surrender. I don't want these men slaughtered."

Sh'sho spoke to his men. There were angry shouts from many of the men, but Sh'sho pointed back at the shore and then at Bolan with his sword. The Pa'ahnuians accepted Sh'sho's words in stony silence. "It shall be as you say."

Bolan turned to the captain. "Get on the intercom. Tell everyone still resisting that I own this ship. Tell them to surrender. Sho, tell your men to accept the surrender of anyone who throws down their weapons and bring them up above deck."

Fighting aboard *The Triple Witch* grudgingly ceased.

Bolan scanned the instruments on the bridge. "What other armament does this ship have?"

Fletcher briefly considered lying, but the time for heroics was over. His duty was clear. He had to save as many of his crew as he could. "You will find two armored boxes up between the sails. They are recessed and disguised as lockers. One is a twin Exocet missile station. The second is a twin Mistral antiaircraft missile launcher. There is a hidden weapons station two decks below. The operator is probably barricaded inside.

"The Papuan blockade vessels have been contacted?"

Fletcher cleared his throat. "Yes."

"Tell your weapons officer I want a firing solution on the incoming ships, and I want the warheads programmed for detonation three hundred yards before impact. I want them driven off, not destroyed."

Fletcher gave the order through the intercom. A very shaky sounding man acknowledged, "Yes, Captain. Radar shows two vessels approaching, ten kilometers out. Preparing firing solution. Warheads programmed to detonate three hundred yards from target."

Bolan nodded. "Launch when ready."

Fletcher punched the intercom button. "Launch when ready."

"Aye-aye, Captain. Ships in range. Firing."

The natives on the deck flinched and crouched as the deck lit up and the two missiles screamed off their twin launch rails. The range was short and they did not need to go into seek mode. They flew straight for their targets trailing smoke and fire.

Bolan watched the proceedings through the cracked glass of the bridge's primary radar display. The radar was not sophisticated enough to pick up the missiles in flight, but the pair of patrol boats were clearly visible as blips on the screen as they closed at full speed.

The weapons officer spoke over the intercom. "Missiles closing. Coming within detonation range. Missiles—"

Twin thunderclaps rolled on the horizon and orange flashes ricocheted off the water as each of the Papuan patrol boats was treated to high explosive detonating directly off their bows.

The message was received loud and clear.

The blips on the radar screen began sharply turning back out into the open ocean.

"Get those launchers reloaded." Bolan looked back through the shattered window at the beach. There were still a very mixed bag of hostiles holding the town.

Sh'sho sighed as he read Bolan's mind. "What do we do? We do not have enough warriors to take them."

"You don't have to. We sank their sub. We have *The Triple Witch*. They're stranded. The Chinese have no business on Pa'ahnui, and they brought weapons of mass destruction with them. Their government will be in face-saving mode. We negotiate with them. We use the Chinese onshore to round up the remaining Russians and pirates for us and put them in holding pens to show the United Nations peacekeeping forces."

"United Nations peace—"

"You need them on this island, Sho, before any other venture capitalist with a brigade of gunmen in his back pocket gets ideas about taking your island. Once the Russians and pirates are rounded up, you give the Chinese every fishing boat with a motor on it and let them sail out of here, on condition they leave their weapons behind."

"Very well." Sh'sho suddenly frowned mightily at Delvoix. "What about him?"

"Him? Calvin and I can't afford to be seen on this island by the UN or the press, but him?" Bolan nodded at the South African mercenary. "Bryce? You want a job?"

Delvoix shrugged. Executive Options had been beheaded, and he was now an unemployed merc short both an arm and an eye. "I have no previous engagements."

"Good. Sh'sho, you're the leader of your people, and Pa'ahnui is free. Here's what I propose you do…"

Epilogue

Church of England

The colonel stepped down nervously from his landing ship onto the beach. He took one look at the reception committee and knew he was in way over his head. Nevertheless, he stood tall in his parade uniform, service medals and blue beret and saluted the man before him. "I am Colonel Dundu Okwudinlo, Kenyan army." He cleared his throat as he stared at the mixture of spears and assault rifles arrayed before him. The only bright point was that the mob was smiling and apparently in good spirits. "Commander of the United Nations peacekeeping forces on the disputed island of Pa'ahnui."

A man in a Che Guevara T-shirt, red star beret and a sarong saluted back. "I am president-elect Bawamuni Sh'sho of the Free Democratic Republic of Pa'ahnui. I welcome you to our island."

"Thank you," the colonel responded warily.

The president gestured back at his entourage. "Let me introduce Patrick Howard Filmoore, Pa'ahnuian representative to the United Nations."

A white man in a crumpled tropical suit with a cattle dog at his feet tipped his floppy hat. "G'day."

"And General Bryce Delvoix, commander in chief of the Free Pa'ahnuian Defense Forces."

Another white man in khaki fatigues missing an arm and an eye saluted. "Colonel, I look forward to cooperating with the United Nations in solving the sovereignty issues confronting this free nation. You may land two platoons onto the beach. Any more will be met with armed resistance."

Colonel Okwudinlo had noted the gigantic beached trimaran on his ride in. He had noted the missile launchers between its sails as well. This was the colonel's first peacekeeping mission. Rumors of sunken Chinese subs, rapacious American billionaires, atrocities against the natives, Filipino pirates and Russian mercenary war criminals had been leaked, along with intriguing supporting evidence, to every news agency on the planet. The "Pa'ahnui Situation" was causing a shit storm in the UN. The newly liberated island of Pa'ahnui had demanded United Nations arbitration and peacekeeping troops to end the violence. They had stated categorically they would kill any nonblack with a weapon that set foot on the beach. The colonel glanced about at all the smiling faces. The violence seemed to have already abated.

The natives appeared to be in total control of their island.